Nancy Drew: Beauty Queen?

Bess bounced up and down in her seat, fishing a pamphlet out of her purse. "You have to compete for Miss Pretty Face!" She handed me the pamphlet.

In the few seconds before the light changed, I read:

Are you the next Miss Pretty Face River Heights? All young women age 16–18 are invited to join our pageant! Compete for scholarships, endorsements, and the opportunity to represent the best in your generation!

"You have got," I said, pulling away as the light changed, "to be kidding."

"Nancy, it's perfect! You qualify, and you're adorable! Plus it would get you right into the middle of things—meeting all the pageant bigwigs, figuring out who had the most to gain!"

I bit my lip.

"You *know* it makes sense," Bess argued. "I could help you, be your fashion coach. I'm sure George would help too. It's a great opportunity! Maybe you'd even win!"

I shuddered. "Nancy Drew, Pageant Girl?"

NANCY DREW

Available from Aladdin Paperbacks

CAROLYN KEENE

NANCY DREW

GIRL DETECTIVE®

PAGEANT PERFECT CRIME

30

Aladdin Paperbacks

New York   London   Toronto   Sydney

This book is a work of fiction. Any references to historical events, real people, or real locales are used fictitiously. Other names, characters, places, and incidents are the product of the author's imagination, and any resemblance to actual events or locales or persons, living or dead, is entirely coincidental.

❦ ALADDIN PAPERBACKS
An imprint of Simon & Schuster Children's Publishing Division
1230 Avenue of the Americas, New York, NY 10020
Copyright © 2008 by Simon & Schuster, Inc.
All rights reserved, including the right of
reproduction in whole or in part in any form.
NANCY DREW, NANCY DREW: GIRL DETECTIVE, ALADDIN PAPER-
BACKS, and related logo are registered trademarks of Simon & Schuster, Inc.
Manufactured in the United States of America
First Aladdin Paperbacks edition June 2008
10 9 8 7 6 5 4 3 2 1
Library of Congress Control Number 2007934377
ISBN-13: 978-1-4169-5528-3
ISBN-10: 1-4169-5528-3

Contents

DETHRONED

"**D**id you miss me?" Ned asked with a grin as he helped me out of my hybrid car. It was a bright sunny day, and I was meeting him at the River Heights University student center after having lunch with him just hours before.

"Oh, terribly," I replied with a smile. "So tell me about this classmate of yours who needs my help."

"Right," said Ned, taking my hand as we walked through the parking lot to the food court entrance. "Her name is Portia Leoni, and she's in my psych class. After our lecture today, she asked to see my notes, and we got to talking. It turns out she's really struggling to pay tuition, because of something that happened to her a few months ago."

I nodded as Ned opened the door for me and we stepped inside. "Something that sounds kind of fishy, you said."

"More than fishy," Ned countered as we walked into the seating area. "It sounded like Portia could use the services of the one, the only . . . "

Suddenly a pretty, petite brunette stood up from her table and started waving at us. "Are you her?" she called to me as we started over. "Are you Nancy Drew?"

I smiled. I do a lot of snooping around, sure, but I didn't know I was famous at the university. "I sure am."

The girl's face erupted into the hugest, whitest smile I'd ever seen. "I'm Portia," she said. "Oh my God, Nancy, I'm so glad you came. When Ned told me he had a friend who investigates things . . . I was, like, 'This could be it,' you know? You could be the answer to all my problems!"

I glanced over at Ned: What had he *told* this girl? Still, it was pretty flattering.

"Um," Ned interrupted as I sat down at the table. "You two get started, but can I get anyone anything? Personally, I could use a cappuccino."

"Oooh, me too," I said.

Portia bit her lip. "Oooh, Neddie, that's so

nice of you. But those have, like, four hundred calories. Can you just get me a Diet Coke?" she asked, reaching over to touch his arm.

Ned quickly backed away. "No problem. Two cappuccinos, one Diet Coke." As he walked over to the coffee stand, I realized what Portia had said: *a friend* who investigates things? I was sure Ned would have mentioned my being his girlfriend. He's about the most solid, stand-up guy you could imagine.

"Anyway," Portia was saying, turning back to me. She had gorgeous dark eyes, done up in a kaleidoscope of eye shadow, that seemed to latch on to mine when she spoke. "I'm sure Ned told you I lost my scholarship."

"He said you were having trouble paying for tuition," I replied.

"Right. Well, the reason for that is I lost my scholarship. And the reason for *that* is . . . " She paused, looking almost disappointed. "Do you not recognize me at all? Really?"

I shook my head.

"Well." Portia sat up straight and sighed a little. "The fact is, I was involved in a local scandal. You've heard of the Miss Pretty Face pageant?"

I shook my head again, but Portia still looked

confused. "I don't really follow pageants," I clarified.

Portia took a good look at me, then pursed her lips and nodded, like it made sense. I wasn't sure whether to feel insulted or not.

"Well," she said, "I won it. I was Miss Pretty Face last year."

"Oh." Right then, Ned came back with our cappuccinos and Portia's Diet Coke. I dove into mine, getting whipped cream on the tip of my nose. Ned laughed and flicked it off with a napkin. Portia didn't look amused.

"So you lost your scholarship when your reign ended?" I asked, trying to get back on track.

"No." Portia leaned over so her eyes bore right into mine. "I was *relieved* of my reign. I was dethroned. And I lost all my winnings, including the scholarship."

"Wow," I breathed, glancing over at Ned. "That's terrible. But why were you—"

"I was set up," Portia broke in before I could finish. "I was dethroned for shoplifting. But I was set up!" She smiled a little rueful smile. "I've never shoplifted in my life."

"So how—," I began.

"I got a call one morning to go to Fleur," she interrupted again. "You've heard of it?"

I shook my head. I had a feeling if I spoke up

again, she'd only cut me off.

"It's a *boutique*," Portia explained, a [...] too slowly. "They sell very upscale cloth...g. Anyway, I was told to go and pick up three dresses for a series of appearances. That kind of thing happens all the time with pageant winners, or any sort of *famou*s people. . . . Stores or designers will loan you clothes to wear, in exchange for free publicity. You mention the store or designer at the event."

I nodded. "Okay. So you went to pick up the dresses, and didn't pay for them?"

Portia nodded furiously. "Which is *normal*. It's totally *normal* in the pageant world. But that night, the police showed up at my house. The *police*."

I nodded. I was pretty friendly with the River Heights police, and it was hard for me to imagine them being scary or intimidating. But I could see why it had upset Portia.

"They *arrested* me," she continued. "For *shoplifting*. And when I got down to the station, they showed me this tape—from Fleur's security cameras. It showed me leaving with the dresses, without paying. And suddenly the shop owner was saying she knew nothing about the whole thing!"

"Maybe she didn't," I suggested. "You said you got a phone call. Maybe she really didn't know anything about the dress pickup."

"But she *did*," Portia insisted, playing with the straw in her soda. "Nancy, I talked to her while I was there. I asked her where the dresses were. And she said, 'Right there on the counter.' She knew what I was talking about."

"Hmmm." I frowned, trying to puzzle this out. Portia took a quick sip of her drink and then beamed at Ned, reaching over to touch his arm again.

"Neddie was so thoughtful and understanding when I told him about this," she said. "He always makes the most insightful comments in class. He's very sensitive."

Ned blushed and cleared his throat, shooting me a look that said, *I wish she'd stop too.*

"Right," I said shortly. "Okay, Portia, I . . ."

What? What was I going to tell her? Her story was interesting, but did I believe it? I try not to judge the people I work for, but I also try not to work for criminals. Portia seemed to be telling the truth, but she could also be a good liar. Was she somebody I'd want to put my reputation behind?

Ned was giving me a thoughtful look. "It's

really the scholarship money that's important," he explained. "I mean, the dethroning, that's embarrassing, right?" He glanced at Portia, who nodded. "But losing the scholarship means Portia might have to drop out of school."

For the first time, Portia looked truly upset. "He's right," she told me softly. "I'm working two jobs right now and still can't keep up with the payments. This isn't just some silly pageant, Nancy: It's my whole *future*."

All right. I'm not made of stone. True, I got a funny vibe off Portia, but really, how much of that was coming from her flirting with Ned? Besides, just because someone annoys you doesn't mean they can't be a crime victim.

"Okay," I said, plopping my empty cappuccino cup down on the table. "I'll stop by Fleur tomorrow, Portia, and do a little snooping. If something seems off, I'll keep investigating. But if they appear to be telling the truth—"

But Portia didn't hear that part. She'd already leaped up from the table and thrown her arms around Ned. "Oh, thank you, thank you, thank you!" she cried. "Neddie, you're the best!"

Ned gave Portia a quick hug and then nudged her away. "Thanks, Nancy," he said with a smile, reaching over and wiping yet more whipped cream off my nose (how did that get there?). "*You're* the best."

I couldn't help smiling back.

"Is it my birthday?" my friend Bess asked, fluffing her hair in the rearview mirror as she slid into the passenger seat of my car. "Do you owe me a favor? Or is it just my lucky day?"

I smiled as I pulled the car back into the street. "Bess, what are you talking about?"

"How many times does *Nancy Drew* call me up and say she wants to go shopping? I'll tell you how many times: never."

"Bess, come on." But I couldn't help smiling a little: Bess was right. She was always decked out in the latest fashions; I was happy if my pants matched my shirt. When Bess talked to me about clothes, she usually had to stop and explain what a "bubble skirt" or an "empire waist" was.

"Let me guess," Bess went on, pausing to turn to me with a mischievous grin that showed her dimples. "You don't *really* want to go shopping. I'm betting you have an ulterior motive—a little snooping to do? Some questions to ask?"

I shook my head and pretended to sigh. "Oh, Bess, you know me too well."

"I was surprised you even knew what Fleur *was*."

I nodded. "Have you shopped there before?"

"Actually I just heard about it." Bess reached into her purse and pulled out a fashion magazine. "*Pose* magazine says it has the best espadrilles for summer. But I never heard a word about it before—you know, before the big scandal."

My mouth dropped open. "You know about the scandal?"

"With Miss Pretty Face and the shoplifting? Sure. Nancy, where have you been?"

I shrugged. I was beginning to wonder how I'd missed out on the River Heights scandal of the year myself. "I guess . . . snooping?"

Bess laughed. "I guess. Seriously, you should make more time to watch the local news. Or at least *Extra.*" She pointed to a small, neatly land-scaped mini-mall on the right. "I think it's in here, way in the back."

I pulled in and we drove around for a while before I realized what Bess meant: *way* in the back, hidden on the other side of the building. Finally, I parked in front of Fleur, a handsome store with two big display windows filled with mannequins in sparkling cocktail dresses.

"So what are you investigating now?" Bess asked, shoving the magazine back into her purse. "A shoplifting ring? A credit card scam?

Is Fleur unwittingly selling counterfeit purses or jewelry?"

I shook my head. "Believe it or not, it's the scandal you mentioned."

"Miss Pretty Face?" Bess looked surprised. "Portia Leoni?"

I nodded.

"I thought that was over and done with," Bess said. "She did it. They caught it on tape. End of story, right?"

I shook my head again. "It's not that simple. She says she had an agreement with the store to borrow the dresses for free publicity. But after she picked them up, the shop owner changed her story. She thinks someone set her up. And if I don't find out who, she might lose her scholarship and have to leave the university."

"Hmmmm." Bess stared at the display window, thoughtful. "Well, if anyone can get to the bottom of this, it's you, Nancy."

Inside, Fleur was abuzz with activity. Businesswomen swished skirts off display racks, high school kids tried on accessories, and an angry mob surrounded the espadrilles, all fighting to grab the ones featured in *Pose* magazine. Bess split off to join the mob as I walked around, getting the lay of the land. I had to admit, a lot of the clothes they carried were really cute. But I *never* would have found this place if Bess hadn't known where to go.

Near the counter, a middle-aged woman with short auburn hair was helping an older woman match a bracelet to a cocktail dress. "We just got these in last week," she said, holding a jet bracelet up to a red-and-black-beaded dress. "I wasn't sure when I ordered them, but in person, they're absolutely gorgeous."

Aha, I thought. If she'd ordered merchandise for the store, she had to be the shop owner, my target.

I lingered around the counter while the older woman bought the dress and bracelet. Then I sauntered over. "Good morning," I said warmly.

"Good morning," the shop owner responded, giving me the once-over. Her voice cooled a bit when she saw my outfit of worn T-shirt and khakis. "I'm Candy. Can I help you with something?"

"I hope so," I said, smiling. "I actually have some questions."

She nodded. "Need help with sizes?"

"Not really," I said, and leaned closer. "I was actually wondering about an incident that happened here. A shoplifting incident. With—"

But Candy's face had already changed, closing off completely. "If you're asking about the Miss Pretty Face scandal, I've already discussed that matter with the police."

I decided to try a different tactic. "Actually, I work for the university bookstore," I lied, "and Ms. Leoni just applied for a position with us. I told her we couldn't possibly hire a shoplifter, but she had a different version of what happened here. She says she was *told* to pick up the dresses by someone from the pageant, and that you seemed to know about that when she came by to get them. Perhaps there was some kind of misunderstanding?" I raised my eyebrows hopefully.

But Candy was having none of this. "Portia Leoni is a liar," she whispered fiercely, looking around the store to see if anyone was watching. "The camera doesn't lie, Ms.—"

"Drew," I supplied.

Candy nodded. "Ms. Drew. I'm not going to discuss this any further. What reason could I possibly have to lie about a theft in my own store?" She looked up at me, but I caught something strange in her expression. Nervousness—almost as though, deep down, she was worried I *might* know a reason she would lie.

"Nobody's calling you a liar," I said carefully. "I just—"

"Good day," Candy spat, and abruptly turned away to approach another customer. "May I help you find a size, miss?"

I stood at the counter for a moment, stunned. Wow. She *really* doesn't want to talk about it, I thought. Here's something funny about people who are telling the truth: They'll talk about anything. Embarrassing incidents, controversies, whatever. A person who's telling the truth has nothing to hide. Liars, on the other hand—they'll avoid the subject at all costs. And half the time, they'll try to make *you* feel bad for bringing it up.

I had a pretty strong suspicion of which category Candy fell into.

I wandered over to find Bess, who was eyeing a butter-colored leather handbag while she chatted with a salesclerk.

". . . one hundred percent leather," the salesclerk was saying. "And if you feel it, you can tell it's of the highest quality."

Bess sighed, running her fingers over the purse's surface. "It is beautiful," she agreed. "It's just a little outside my price range. Do you think it might go on sale soon?"

The salesclerk—her nametag said DAHLIA—shook her head, looking apologetic. "Probably not," she advised with a little shrug of her shoulders. "Business has been so busy lately. We haven't had a sale since . . . well, since before that Miss Pretty Face thing."

Hmmmm. I leaned in.

"So business picked up after that?" Bess prompted.

Dahlia nodded. "Oh yeah, tons. It went from being dead in here to being packed, all the time. In fact"—she glanced over at Candy, saw that she was still busy helping the woman she'd left me for, and lowered her voice—"it's kind of weird, but before the shoplifting? We were told the store might close at the end of the month. With this lousy location, we couldn't get any customers."

Bess turned to meet my eye. I could tell she knew I was putting something together.

"Hmmm," she said, stroking the purse one last time. "Well, thanks for your help, Dahlia. I'm going to pass on the purse today. But congrats on the great business—I'll have to come back and check out your new stock next week."

Dahlia smiled, took the purse back, and then turned to help another customer. I gave Bess a little nod, and we strolled out of the store and back to my car and climbed in. Still thinking it over, I turned the key in the ignition.

"So," said Bess with an expectant look. "Any helpful info?"

I nodded slowly. "The owner sticks to her story, that it was a shoplifting," I said. "But there's something off about her. She seemed tense—like she had something to hide."

Bess nodded. "And what Dahlia said?" she said. "About the store almost closing? I could see all the gears turning in your mind."

I smiled. "It's odd, isn't it? The store was losing money until Portia supposedly shoplifted, and then all of a sudden business was booming."

"What do you think it means?" Bess asked.

I sighed. "Maybe someone paid Fleur's owner to accuse Portia of shoplifting," I replied. "If they were losing money and the store was about to close, that makes them ripe for a bribe."

"Hmmm." Bess reached out and tapped her fingers on the dash. "So what are you going to do?"

"I don't know," I admitted. "It's possible that someone *did* set Portia up. But who, and why? And how can I even figure out the answers to any of these questions when I know nothing about the pageant itself?"

I drove a bit, and suddenly became aware of a change in Bess's expression. She was staring at me, grinning. When I turned and looked at her at a stoplight, she looked like she was about to explode—like Christmas, her birthday, and a half-off sale at Macy's had all arrived on the same day, right then.

"*Nancy*," she said. "You know what you have to do?"

I shook my head. "What?"

Bess bounced up and down in her seat, fishing a pamphlet out of her purse. "You have to compete for Miss Pretty Face!"

She handed me the pamphlet. In the few seconds before the light changed, I read:

Are you the next Miss Pretty Face River Heights? All young women age 16–18 are invited to join our pageant! Compete for scholarships, endorsements, and the opportunity to represent the best in your generation!

"You have got," I said, pulling away as the light changed, "to be kidding."

"Nancy, it's perfect! You qualify, and you're adorable! Plus, it would get you right into the middle of things—meeting all the pageant bigwigs, figuring out who had the most to gain!"

I bit my lip.

"You *know* it makes sense," Bess argued. "I could help you, be your fashion coach. I'm sure George would help too. It's a great opportunity! Maybe you'd even win!"

I shuddered. "Nancy Drew, Pageant Girl?"

Bess rolled her eyes. "Don't be a snob, Nancy. Come on."

I sighed, pulling up to Bess's house. I'm about the least pageanty person in the universe—I hardly ever wear makeup, and I doubt "snooping" counts toward the talent competition. I tried to picture myself up on a stage, huge hair, sparkly dress, blinding smile, crying demurely as a tiara was placed on my head.

Not that I'd *ever* win.

I looked at Bess, who was looking at me with that excited, expectant look. If this was Christmas morning, I had become Bess's Santa Claus.

"All right," I said, covering my ears to block out Bess's shriek of joy. "I'll do it."

2

PRETTY SUSPICIOUS

"This is such bunk," my friend George fumed as she, Bess, and I entered the Mahoney Community Center a few days later. All around the lobby, huge posters announced the Miss Pretty Face pageant, and a flock of beautiful girls wandered around, flanked by their mothers or boyfriends or friends.

"It's *not* bunk," Bess replied, with the wary-but-patient tone of someone who expected this very argument. Bess and George are cousins, but they're polar opposites in almost every way—including how they feel about pageants. "Pageants are empowering to women, George. They reward intelligence and poise and they pay millions of dollars in tuition scholarships each year."

George snorted. "Yeah, as long as you have no cellulite and know how to walk in an evening gown and heels," she muttered. "That's the problem, Bess: Pageants tell women there's a *right* way to be a woman, and a *wrong* way. All the intelligence in the world won't win the pageant if it doesn't come with a perfect body and a white smile."

Bess glared at her cousin. "Oh, come *on*—"

"Truce!" I yelled, holding up my hands in a T-shape. "Truce! Look, we're not here to debate whether pageants are good or not. We're here to sign me up so I can start snooping. Anyone see a sign-in?"

George looked around and pointed to a table set up outside the center's gymnasium. "There?"

"Thanks." I led them over to the sign-up table. A woman in her mid-forties with bleached-blond hair sat behind the table, handing out clipboards. "I'd like to sign in, please?"

The woman glanced up at me and gave me a quick once-over, the corners of her mouth wrinkling in disapproval. In my track pants and hoodie, with my hair up in a messy ponytail, I *did* look pretty different from the perfectly tailored young women who wandered around inside the gym. But what did they expect? The pamphlet had said there would be a dance rehearsal today—"please be ready to move."

Actually, everyone else seemed to be carrying gym bags, probably containing their workout clothes.

Oops.

The woman's face cracked into a faux smile and she handed me a clipboard. "Welcome. I'm Cupcake Hughes, Miss Pretty Face 1982. I'll be your coach and choreographer this year. Please fill out these forms."

"Thanks." I took the clipboard and walked with George and Bess over to the bleachers, where I began filling in the information.

"Seriously, Nancy," George said, watching a gaggle of contestants greet one another with huge smiles. "*You're* not into pageants, are you? Deep down, you know this whole thing is ridiculous."

"I'm not sure," I answered George honestly. I read a question on the form—WHY DO YOU WANT TO BE MISS PRETTY FACE?—and paused, pen poised over the paper. To catch a crook? Probably not the answer they were looking for. Finally I filled in, "To learn more about pageants and what I am capable of."

"Ladies!" Cupcake was suddenly shouting,

moving to the center of the gym. "I need all friends and family to leave now. Thank you for your support of these beautiful girls. But we need to get down to business—and start preparing your girls to be Miss Pretty Face!"

There was a smattering of applause, and the mothers, grandmothers, and friends started filtering out of the room. I turned to George and Bess. Bess looked at me like I was about to accept my Nobel Prize. George looked at me like I was about to be boiled in oil.

"Thanks for coming with me, guys," I said, standing up with my clipboard. "But I guess it's time for the action to start."

"Good luck," Bess said excitedly.

"Good luck," George echoed flatly, and they both turned to head out the exit.

So: Down to business. I walked over to the middle of the gym, where Cupcake was standing in a huddle of contestants. It seemed like I was one of the last contestants to arrive, and many of the other girls were already deep in conversation. I looked them over, sizing up my fellow contestants: twelve girls, nine of which were blond; lots of bubbly cheerleader types; I was the only one with even a hint of red in my hair. I fiddled with my strawberry blond ponytail nervously, suddenly feeling like this was a junior high cafeteria and I was the new girl with no place to sit.

"Nancy?"

I startled at the sound of a familiar voice.

"Deirdre?"

A familiar brunette approached me, her face an expression of surprise.

"Wow," Deirdre murmured, "I never would have pegged you to enter a beauty contest, Nancy."

I tried to smile. I've known Deirdre for years. She's not a bad person, deep down inside. But she sometimes has trouble seeing the world beyond her own nose.

"I'm turning over a new leaf," I said brightly. "Isn't this fun?"

Deirdre smiled tightly. Behind her, a couple of blondes had turned to watch our conversation.

"Deirdre?" asked the taller one, the lighter blonde. "Is this a friend of yours?"

Deirdre let out an almost-imperceptible sigh before turning back to the blondes. "Girls, let me introduce you to Nancy Drew. Nancy and I went to school together. And apparently she now wants to compete in pageants."

The shorter, darker blonde smiled. "Is this your first pageant?" she asked me.

"It sure is," I replied.

Both girls looked me over, head to toe.

"Well, how nice that you're giving pageants a try," said the taller blonde. "I'm Fallon, by the way. Fallon Gregory. Get used to that name—because you're going to hear it called when the new Miss Pretty Face is announced."

My jaw almost dropped. Did all beauty queens talk like this?

The darker blonde shot me an apologetic look. "Don't be offended. Fallon's just super confident. And she really wants to win this year because she had to drop out last year."

"You did?" I asked Fallon.

"I got mono," she said coolly. "But I already had all my dresses bought, and my whole talent routine worked out. And not to brag or anything, but I was the front-runner." Fallon smiled. She had a dazzling, perfect toothpaste-commercial smile. Exactly the kind of smile you'd expect a pageant queen to have.

The shorter girl held out her hand to me. "I'm Piper Depken," she said as I took her hand and shook it. "This is only my third pageant. I'm no pro like Fallon. But I would really love to win, or at least *place*. . . . I could really use the scholarship money."

Deirdre turned to meet my eye, still with the

same tight smile. "Piper lives in Havenwood."

Havenwood was a low-income apartment complex on a nonglamorous bank of the river. Deirdre might as well have told me, *Piper's poor.*

I smiled at Piper. "Well, I hope you win it," I said honestly.

"Thanks," she said, hesitation flashing across her face. "Nancy, I like you. Can I tell you something?"

Tell me something? My heart raced as I wondered if this might be related to Portia's dethroning. "Of course you can. What?"

Piper leaned in, lowering her voice as she whispered to me. "You need to lose at least ten pounds, honey."

My stomach fell. *What?*

"If you want to win," Piper added quickly. "I don't want to hurt your feelings. I'm just telling you what I see. But you know what?"

"What?" I asked, still trying to make sense of her advice. Lose ten pounds? I may not be some wan-looking supermodel, but I am *perfectly* healthy, I can tell you that much.

"I'm going to start the Master Cleanse tomorrow," Piper went on whispering, a smile blossoming across her face. "You should do it with me! We'll both slim down fast. You know,

I heard it's what Beyoncé did to slim down for *Dreamgirls*!"

The Master Cleanse? I bit my lip to keep from making a face. Bess had read me an article from one of her magazines about the Master Cleanse—basically, you eat nothing for ten days except a weird concoction of lemon juice, maple syrup, and cayenne pepper. It's supposed to "cleanse" your system, so you lose weight. Of course, almost all doctors think it's ridiculous and just another silly way for women to starve themselves. I was tempted to tell Piper the truth—but I also wondered if pretending to do the Cleanse with her would make us closer, and hopefully get me some useful information.

"Huh," I said. "That sounds like it may be fun. Can you bring the stuff tomorrow?"

"Sure!" Piper's smile expanded so much that I felt a little guilty. She seemed honestly excited. "Girl, we *have* to do whatever we can to win the title of Miss Pretty Face. Have you heard about the prizes?"

"Prizes?" I echoed as Deirdre and Fallon looked on curiously. "Sure. I mean, I know about the scholarships. What else is there?"

"What *else*?" Fallon snorted. "The scholarships are just the beginning. Miss Pretty Face River

Heights gets a $1,000 cash prize. Free cosmetics for life. A new car, yours to keep even after your reign ends. A free trip to New York City to compete in the national pageant, just a couple weeks away. Plus you get a contract with Pretty Face Cosmetics to promote their products, and you get paid extra for that." She looked down her nose at me. "This pageant is serious business, Nancy. If you want to win . . . you'd better get serious."

Serious. Right. My mind was racing—those prizes really were *spectacular*. Spectacular enough to set someone up in order to get them. When Portia had been dethroned, the runner-up must have taken her place—getting the crown, *and* all Portia's prizes. That was a pretty *serious* motive. I wanted to ask who the runner-up was last year, but I reminded myself that I was supposed to look like a contestant right now, not a detective.

"Girls?" Cupcake shouted, standing in the middle of the gym. "Let's settle down, please. I need everyone in horizontal rows of six, right in front of me."

All of the girls slowly walked over and formed rows, grumbling at Cupcake's drill-sergeant tone.

As I took my place in the first row, I noticed

a middle-aged man walking from the side of the gym to join Cupcake. He was handsome, in a dad sort of way: wavy brown hair with a dusting of gray; warm blue eyes; trim physique dressed in an expensive-looking tailored suit. I wondered if he was a pageant bigwig.

"This is Kyle McMahon," Cupcake announced, smiling and gesturing as Kyle reached her side. "He's the regional vice president of Pretty Face Cosmetics, and the overseer of our regional pageant. Let's all say hello to Kyle."

Everyone said a quiet "hello" or "hi, Kyle."

"Hello, ladies," Kyle greeted us. His voice was deep and welcoming. "I'd like to thank you for taking part in this year's competition. As you know, the pageant is sponsored by Pretty Face Cosmetics, the cosmetics company that cares."

"It's very important to showcase our products during this pageant," Kyle went on, "which is why you'll all be asked to wear Pretty Face Cosmetics on all your pretty faces." A few girls giggled. "This year, we'll be showcasing our newest product, Perfect Face." Kyle reached into his pocket and pulled out a tiny pink tube. "Perfect Face is a moisturizer and skin revitalizer. It reduces signs of aging, provides SPF protection, and gives you a shimmery glow. Once you ladies try this on your faces, I'm sure you'll want to wear it all the time. But it's very important for you to always be wearing it during the pageant."

All the girls whispered excitedly, peering over at the pink tube in Kyle's hand.

"To practice, we'll be wearing it during all rehearsals," Cupcake added. "You girls will find a box of the latest Pretty Face Cosmetics, including a tube of Perfect Face, on each dressing table."

The excited noises from the girls grew louder now, and I realized, once again, how out of place I was here.

Kyle continued. "Please remember to wear it. Don't forget, you're not just competing in a beauty pageant, you're also representing all of us who work at Pretty Face Cosmetics. If any of you have any questions, feel free to contact me. Otherwise, good luck, and thank you for participating."

Everyone applauded as Kyle smiled, gave a last wave, and headed for the exit. As he walked off, Cupcake took his position, raised a whistle to her lips, and blew an earsplitting sound.

"All right!" she shouted. "I need quiet! And when I mean quiet, I mean dead silence! I take this pageant seriously, and you should too! Now let's get down to business."

I glanced at the girl next to me: *Is she for real?* She just nodded and shrugged.

Great, I thought. Let's get down to business.

"Did you misunderstand the rules?" Cupcake asked me in a shocked tone a few hours later. We were standing on the Center's auditorium stage outside the dressing room, where all of my competitors were changing into their gym clothes. I, of course, was already in my sweats and ready to go—except Cupcake had just swooped over to inform me that my sneakers were all wrong. The rules specifically instructed contestants to bring "white-soled tennis shoes"—and my sneakers had black bottoms.

Oops.

"I'm so sorry," I babbled. I'd been apologizing for five minutes. "I did read the rules. I'm just new to this pageant business, and I guess I was so nervous about competing that the part about white soles slipped my mind."

"I'm not sure how you'll do as a contestant, Nancy, if you can't understand even these basic guidelines." Cupcake's mouth creased into a frown, and I could see lines sprouting from the corners. "First, you flubbed your introduction." True. You were supposed to say, "My name is so-and-so, I live on so-and-so street, and I enjoy such-and-such activity!" I'd panicked and said, "My name is River Court, I live on Nancy Drew, and I like pineapples!" Which is true—the part about the pineapples, anyway—and yet totally wrong.

"*Then* you bumped into Kendra and Yvonne during the promenade."

Also true. I'd caused an embarrassing domino effect that had almost toppled the whole line. Fortunately, my competitors were much swifter on their feet than I was.

"I just don't *know*, Nancy, if pageants are for you." Cupcake sighed and shook her head. I wanted to agree with her, but I knew I couldn't. I had to stay in the pageant if I wanted to get to the bottom of whatever had happened to Portia.

"I'm learning fast, Cupcake, I promise I am," I argued. "Tomorrow I'll be a whole new Nancy. Can't I just practice in these sneakers today, and tomorrow I'll bring white-soled ones?"

Cupcake blanched. "Absolutely *not*. You'd scuff the stage, and the Mahoney Community Center shouldn't have to deal with that. You can't take part in the dance rehearsal unless you find a pair of white-soled tennis shoes, *as it says in the rules*."

A petite, blond-ponytailed contestant stepped out of the dressing room in red track shorts and a tank top. I wasn't sure what her name was, but I'd caught her shooting me some sympathetic glances each time I'd messed up earlier. She seemed to have caught the tail end of Cupcake's speech.

"What's going on?" she asked. "Anything I can help with?"

"I very much doubt that," said Cupcake. "Nancy has brought the wrong shoes to rehearsal."

The girl glanced down at my feet. "Oh, that's a shame. What size do you wear, Nancy?"

"A seven and a half."

The girl glanced up at me and smiled, revealing pretty, white teeth and cute, lopsided dimples. "Well, you're in luck. I just got new tennies, and my old ones are still in my gym bag. I wear an eight, but if you don't mind wearing them, they should get you through the first rehearsal."

I let out a sigh of relief. "Oh, my gosh, thank you!"

"Of course. I'm Kelly, by the way. Come with me."

I glanced back at Cupcake, who just shrugged and gestured for me to follow Kelly. Thankful, I turned and followed my Good Samaritan back to the dressing room.

"Wow," I said softly as she walked me to a dressing station near the front of the room, on the opposite side from the one I'd been assigned. "You are a *life*saver. I can't thank you enough. I think Cupcake was about to tell me to hit the road and never come back."

Kelly laughed a light, bell-like laugh. "Don't take it personally," she said, leaning down to pull some pink-and-white sneakers out of her gym bag. "Cupcake's been working this pageant for the last ten years and she's just like that, tough on everybody." She shrugged. "I guess she just takes the pageant really seriously. But it can be a little intimidating when you're new."

I nodded. "I'm definitely feeling intimidated."

Kelly laughed again. "Don't be. It's just a beauty pageant—not brain surgery."

I smiled. Kelly seemed nice and down to earth, much less intense than the girls I'd met this morning. "Is this your first pageant too?"

Kelly shook her head. "My second."

"So you were here last year?"

Kelly nodded. After looking at me for a moment, she reached down to her gym bag and started fishing around again. "I didn't win," she said, grabbing something and pulling it out. "But after Portia was dethroned?" She pulled the item out of the bag and I saw it for the first time: It was a tiara, huge and sparkly. She placed it on her head and posed, holding a pretend bouquet against her chest. "I guess you could say I learned fast."

My mouth dropped open. "*You're* the current Miss Pretty Face?"

Kelly smiled again, looking a little embarrassed as she took the tiara off and put it back in the bag. "I'm lucky, is what I am. But, yeah—that too. Miss Pretty Face by default."

I didn't know what to say. If Kelly was last year's runner-up—and everything Piper had said earlier about the prizes was true—then I was looking at my number-one suspect. Nobody had more motive to get Portia out of the picture than last year's runner-up. But was that possible? Kelly just seemed so . . . *nice.*

I tried to pull myself together. Plenty of times, seemingly nice people do bad things. I knew this deep down. It was just hard to imagine Kelly acting cutthroat. With her tiny frame and her curly blond ponytail, she seemed about as cutthroat as a toy poodle.

"Anyway," I said, standing up, "thank you so much. For the sneakers. And congrats."

Kelly just winked at me. "Forget about it," she

said. "Make it worth my while by turning into an awesome competitor and surprising the heck out of the girls who've been doing this for years." With one last smile, she turned and headed out of the dressing room. I noticed a tiny pink phone sitting on a chair just inside the dressing room. Kelly's phone! I walked over, grabbed it, and shoved it into my pocket. I'm no thief, but I'm not above borrowing small things if it will give me an excuse to look up a person later—and maybe get a look at their personal space.

Yup, I thought as I followed Kelly out to the auditorium. I think I have to get to know Kelly a little better.

3

PHONE TRAIL

"This is highly irregular, Nancy," Cupcake Hughes explained over the phone. "I wish you had just told me during rehearsal that you found Kelly's cell phone."

"I didn't find it until I was in the parking lot," I replied innocently. "She was wearing it on a clip at her waist. It must have just fallen off. I want to get it back to her tonight—I know how important cell phones can be."

Cupcake sighed. "In my day, if you couldn't reach a person for a few hours, life went on," she huffed. But I could hear her rustling papers in the background. "All right. Here it is. Kelly lives at 23 Ryan Road." She paused. "Did you get that?"

I scribbled the address on a note on my dash. "Yes, thank you so much."

"You're welcome. And Nancy?"

"Yes?" I said, throwing my pencil back into the glove compartment and placing the note on the passenger seat.

"Don't forget those new sneakers tomorrow." Click. I smiled, flipping on my headlights and putting my car into gear.

I'd just finished up dinner with Hannah, our housekeeper, and Dad, and the town was bathed in the warm pink light of sunset. I drove slowly over to Ryan Road, a quiet street several blocks from downtown that held a number of neat, older houses. When I got there, I saw that number 23 was a large, stately redbrick house. Hmmmm. If Kelly *had* sabotaged Portia to get the crown, it looked like she didn't do it because she needed the money.

I parked in the street, grabbing Kelly's tiny pink phone from the passenger seat and heading up to the front door. Snooping around often forces me to tell fibs, but I find it easier when I have a prop in my hand. Somehow it seems much more plausible to hand someone their phone and explain that you found it than it does to just show up on their doorstep with some crazy excuse.

I knocked on the door and set my face in a bright smile. *Hi, Kelly,* I rehearsed. *I'm sure you're surprised to see me here. It's just that I guess you dropped your phone at rehearsal, so I picked it up for you. Your address? Oh, I called Cupcake and . . .*

"Can I help you?" A handsome, middle-aged man was standing at the front door, looking puzzled. Actually, a familiar, handsome, middle-aged man. *Actually*—

"Kyle McMahon!" I blurted. And just like that, the whole case turned on its head.

"I'm sure Kelly won't be long," Kyle told me warmly, flipping a dish towel over his arm. "She was just going to get a DVD for us to watch and some popcorn."

We were standing in a large, well-appointed foyer of what looked like a beautiful—and expensively decorated—house. A sunken living room off to our right was furnished with oversize ivory furniture, and a wide, wood-paneled stairway led up to a skylit balcony with hallways off to either side.

"May I use your bathroom while I wait?" I asked hopefully, glancing up the stairway.

"Of course!" Kyle smiled and headed back to the kitchen. "Upstairs, second door on your right."

"Thanks." I quickly and quietly climbed the stairs, thick carpet muffling my footsteps. My mind was racing. Kyle McMahon was Kelly's father. The current Miss Pretty Face was the daughter of an employee. Wasn't that strange?

I turned right and spotted the bathroom right away, just where Kyle had told me it was. Beyond that, a door opened onto a light lavender bedroom. I stepped into the doorway, hoping it would be Kelly's. *Bingo*. Posters and photos lined the walls, and girlish lavender ruffles covered a neat twin bed. This *had* to be Kelly's room.

I stepped in hesitantly. I didn't have very much time, but I still felt strange investigating Kelly—a person who had been nothing but nice to me. Still, I looked all around the walls: #1 CHEERLEADER AWARD. A poster of Orlando Bloom. A pendant for River Heights University. And photos—so many photos.

Most of them were of Kelly and her friends. Kelly and a group of pretty girls in caps and gowns, smiling earnestly. Kelly and a handsome red-haired boy, dressed up and posing in front of the fireplace before what looked to be their prom. Kelly and—*oh my gosh*.

I carefully pulled the photo from the wall, careful not to tear the tape. In the center stood Kelly, smiling a little self-consciously in the same dress she wore in the prom photo. Her hair was down and she wore little makeup, like she was trying the dress on for the first time. On her left side, with his arm tight around Kelly and wearing a big, proud smile, was Kyle. And on her other side, looking less enthused but much happier than when I'd seen her, was the owner of Fleur.

They know each other. If Kyle and Kelly knew Candy—then that meant they had the means to get Portia dethroned. It looked like they were good friends. Maybe all it had taken was a phone call—a quick discussion, laying out the plan and how good it might be for Fleur's business. Turning on the security camera, calling Portia, and *bingo*—a whole new Miss Pretty Face.

I turned and walked over to Kelly's bureau. It was littered with cards and more photos. One card stood out as bigger than all the others—it was thick cream paper, edged with pink, and it bore a huge gold CONGRATULATIONS.

I picked up the card and opened it up. "Kelly, you've always been my Pretty Face, but now it's time to show the world. You didn't win the first time around, but now we know the prettiest girl has the crown. Use it well, and remember that I'll always love you. Hugs and kisses, Dad."

Hmmmm. Just as I was about to slip the card into my purse, a familiar bell-like voice shattered the silence.

"Well, Nancy Drew," Kelly's voice greeted me from just a few feet behind me. "Fancy meeting you here."

4

ALL MADE UP

I gulped, and quickly pasted a huge grin on my face. "Kelly!" I squealed, trying to sound as excited as if I'd been waiting for her all day. "I'm so glad to see you! I was on my way to the bathroom, but then I got distracted by the"—I searched the room wildly, trying not to let Kelly see my panic—"paintings!"

I pointed, thrilled to have found an object that might have attracted my attention. Four small square paintings hung over Kelly's bed, a quartet of bright, abstract oils that picked up the lavender and sea colors of her bedroom.

"They're so lovely," I gushed. They *were* awfully pretty, actually. "Did you paint them?"

"No," Kelly said, stepping closer. Her face had

softened into a sad smile and if she remained suspicious to find me in her bedroom, her expression didn't show it. "My mother painted those. Aren't they special?"

"I love the colors," I agreed. Slipping my hand into my pocket, I extracted Kelly's cell phone and held it out to her. "Your dad probably told you why I'm here. I found this after rehearsal today, and I didn't want you to go without it until tomorrow. I know I'm lost without mine."

Kelly nodded and smiled more brightly, taking the phone. "Thanks, Nancy," she said, giving me a thoughtful look. "Actually, I'm glad you came over. You seem like a nice person. I hope this doesn't sound too dorky, but I'm glad to get to hang out more."

Kelly sounded warm and sincere. But she was so pretty and sweet—why would a beauty contest winner be so thrilled to make a potential friend? Didn't she have a lot of friends already?

"I'm glad too," I agreed. "You were so nice to lend me your sneakers this morning. Maybe I could stay a bit and you could give me some more pageant tips?"

Kelly nodded. "That sounds great! I'll go tell Dad you're staying and that we can watch the movie tomorrow. Want some popcorn?"

I nodded. "That sounds fantastic."

"Awesome." Kelly smiled again, showing her lopsided dimples. "I'll be right back." She left the room and soon I heard her muffled footsteps heading down the stairs.

Stealthily, I walked back to the bureau and grabbed the card from Kyle. " . . . the prettiest girl has the crown," I read again. Was it possible? Could Kelly have arranged for Portia to be set up? I knew I was letting my own feelings get in the way of good sleuthing, but I just couldn't imagine sweet, earnest Kelly taking part in such things. Either she was a great actress, or . . .

Or.

I looked at Kelly's wall of photos again. Every third or fourth photo had her dad in it—smiling, hugging Kelly, looking incredibly proud as she graduated high school or won a tennis match or turned sixteen. It looked like they were close—after all, how many teenage girls spent a summer night watching a DVD with their fathers? Not many. Could it be that Kelly wasn't behind the dethroning—but Kyle was? That he had manipulated the pageant behind the scenes to see his beloved daughter get what he thought was her due?

"All right," Kelly announced from behind me,

sweeping back into the room with a big bowl of popcorn. "Dad seemed disappointed, but he'll get over it. He doesn't like me to go out late at night, but with the two of us being right here, under the same roof, there's not much he can complain about." Kelly looked up and smiled sheepishly, sitting down on her bed. "What's your dad like? Is he crazy protective too?"

"I think all dads want to protect their little girls," I said, sitting down to join her. "Though, actually, Dad gives me a lot of freedom. He trusts me a lot—and I do everything I can to earn that trust."

I gestured to the photo of Kelly, her dad, and the owner of Fleur, hoping to get an explanation of their relationship. "Is that your mother?"

"Oh, no," Kelly replied. Either I was crazy, or an expression of extreme distaste flashed over her face, like she didn't like this woman. She recovered quickly, though. "That's Candy Hokanson. She's an old family friend, nothing more. No, my mom died when I was ten." Kelly's voice softened as she said this, like it was still a little hard for her to say.

"I'm sorry," I said honestly. "My mom died when I was little too."

Kelly nodded. "I still miss her," she admitted.

"Sometimes I think if she was still alive, my dad would be a little less strict."

I nodded. "Maybe," I agreed. "Maybe since he lost one person, he's really concerned with keeping you safe."

Kelly nodded again, more slowly. "Oh, well," she said. "I'm not complaining. I get along pretty well with Dad, and at least I know he cares." She paused, standing up and walking over to a vanity that was bursting with cosmetics. "Besides," she said with a mischievous smile, "he gets me all kinds of great cosmetics for free. Check this out, Nancy."

I stood up and followed her, looking over the collection with a low whistle. "This is amazing," I told her. "There are products here I didn't even know existed!"

"Some of them don't," Kelly explained, picking up a creamy metallic purple eyeshadow. "Not at the retail level, anyway. This, for example? They tested it in a cream shadow, but a focus group said they preferred it as an eyeliner."

"Wow," I said. "You must have the definitive Pretty Face collection! My friend Bess would freak out."

"She can come over anytime," Kelly suggested. "I have so much, I couldn't possibly use it all! I'm happy to share."

I picked up a small white box with pink roses all over it and a woman's profile embossed on the top. Carefully opening the flap, I removed a small glass bottle of white cream. "Hey!" I cried, reading the label on the box. "'Perfect Face Moisturizer and Face Revitalizer'! But this isn't the kind we have at the pageant."

"Ooh!" Kelly cried, taking the box from me and reading it. "You're right. The stuff sold in stores is in a little tube, right?"

"And it's pink," I added, opening the tiny bottle and taking a whiff. "And it smells like roses. This stuff smells kind of like . . . cake."

Kelly sniffed delicately. "Vanilla," she corrected. "It was the *it* fragrance a few years ago. This is my dad's job—test the products and then tell the scientists they have to switch from a vanilla scent to rose, because rose is the *it* scent now. Isn't it funny?"

I grinned. But then I realized, again, that Kyle was a bigwig in the Pretty Face company—and Kelly was Miss Pretty Face. Coincidence? "Kelly," I said gently, trying to look curious and not suspicious, "don't take this the wrong way, but does it happen often that an employee's daughter wins the crown in the Miss Pretty Face Pageant? I mean"—I rushed to amend myself, seeing Kelly's smile fade—"*I* know you would never be involved in any foul play. I've only known you a few hours, but I believe that. I guess I'm just surprised that you were allowed to compete."

Kelly nodded, looking a little less upset. "Well, in terms of the pageant, Pretty Face believes that 'all girls have the right to feel beautiful.'" She rolled her eyes. "My dad quoted that to me a million times. The truth is, I didn't even want to enter the pageant—he thought it would be a good experience." She sighed. "And it has been, mostly. In terms of the rules, though, *everyone* is allowed to compete—they just make sure that none of the judges are Pretty Face employees. It's a little unusual, but then it's a fairly small pageant, so they play by their own rules."

Interesting. And very interesting that Kyle was more interested in Kelly competing than she was.

We continued to dig through the pile of cosmetics, Kelly pausing to show me products she especially liked or knew some funny inside story about. I didn't even care about makeup that much, but I had to admit, this was turning out to be fun.

When we'd finally looked through everything,

I turned to Kelly. "Amazing," I said. "It's a treasure trove, Kelly. What could you possibly do with all these cosmetics?"

Kelly just smiled slyly, reaching over to push my hair out of my face and holding up some pink eyeshadow. "How about a makeover?"

Amazingly—to me, at least—Kelly's pile of cosmetics hadn't left me looking like a clown. In fact, her makeup job was natural and flattering. My blue eyes stood out beautifully under some soft taupe and pink shadow, and a rose-colored sheer lipstick accentuated my mouth. As she worked, Kelly explained how I could create the same look on myself for the pageant, and she was even nice enough to *give* me the colors she'd used when she was finished.

"Oh, Kelly, I couldn't possibly!" I protested, staring at the glamorous stranger in the mirror.

"Don't be silly," she said, dropping the cosmetics into my bag. "I can get replacements. I have connections. Besides, anything I can do to help a nice girl win Miss Pretty Face is my pleasure."

I laughed. "If today's rehearsal is any indication, I think you may be wasting your time."

Kelly just shook her head. "Don't sell yourself short, Nancy Drew."

When I left the McMahon house, I looked like a new and improved version of myself. Sitting in my car and thinking over the events of the night, it was harder than ever to imagine Kelly having anything to do with Portia's scandal. But I forced myself to keep the option open. It was possible that there were two sides to Kelly. Still, as I pulled my car into the street and headed home, I hoped against hope that if any McMahons were involved in the setup, it would be Kyle.

NUMBER-ONE SUSPECT

I moaned as I stretched my back in the dressing room the next day, running my fingers through my hair and trying to recover from another crushing day of rehearsal. Dance routines, endless choreography for just getting on and off stage, and even talent rehearsal. Against my better judgment, I was singing "On My Own" from *Les Misérables*—because Cupcake said that singing was "the go-to talent for girls with no discernable talent." Besides, it wasn't as though I could get up on stage and dust the microphones for fingerprints. In beauty pageants, amateur sleuthing didn't count as a "talent."

Who knew beauty pageants were such hard work?

And even now that we were finished, Cupcake was reminding us to keep practicing all day. "Girls, keep rehearsing that hop-turn-kick move and the 'star' as best you can alone," she encouraged. "And remember to eat right, and cut back on the salt so you don't retain water for the pageant. No matter what you do, don't skimp on those workouts!"

I cringed. Workouts, on top of this nightmare? She must be kidding. My plan for the rest of the whole day was nap, nap, and, if I had time after my nap, have ice cream. But I guessed that was why I wasn't a beauty queen. "You *must* be kidding," I murmured to myself.

"She's *not*." Fallon, Piper, and Deirdre suddenly appeared at my side, all looking fresh as daisies. How were they not exhausted after that grueling rehearsal? Fallon continued: "Pageants are hard work, Nancy. Your practice time shouldn't end once you leave the auditorium. *Real* beauty queens eat, sleep, and breathe the pageant until the crown is theirs."

I just stared at Fallon, too tired to be offended. "Wow."

Deirdre tossed her hair. "Isn't this fun, Nancy? I feel totally reinvigorated after that rehearsal. I almost can't believe I haven't entered a pageant before."

I nodded. "Me either." In fact, Deirdre was shaping into a surprisingly tough competitor.

"Nancy!" Piper broke in, smiling widely and pushing a jar of murky copper-colored liquid in my direction. "Girl, I promised and now I'm delivering! Will you really stick to this and take it seriously? Will you?"

"I will!" I promised automatically, not quite sure what I was agreeing to. Stick to the pageant and take it seriously? Stick to . . .

"The Master Cleanse," Piper announced, and my stomach dropped, "is a detox program that will make you feel stronger, happier, and more energized." She grinned. "And the most important thing, ten pounds thinner! Girl, you don't want those love handles showing through your bathing suit." Before I could stop her, she reached out and grabbed a little pinch of my belly, squeezing it between her fingers. "I'm not trying to be mean! I'm only telling you because I love!"

"Um, thanks," I said, trying to smile. "I . . . I do appreciate this, Piper."

Piper beamed. "No problem, girlfriend. I could see you needed help."

"You'll have to tell me how it works, Nancy." Deirdre smirked in my direction.

I shook the jug of "lemonade." The murky

liquid churned around, and a few red grains of pepper floated ominously to the surface. I felt a flash of pity for Piper, knowing that she would actually be drinking this.

Fallon grinned. "Tough luck about that singing thing, by the way. I'm sure you'll . . . figure something out."

I nodded. Even though she'd recommended I try singing, Cupcake had said my rendition of "On My Own" was "about as pleasing to the ears as a vacuum cleaner." But I wasn't worried. She'd given me a few pointers on building up my voice. Besides, as long as nobody suffered permanent ear damage, I just wanted to get through this pageant in one piece.

"So how often do I drink this?" I asked Piper.

"As much as you want!" Piper explained happily. "I can make you more, if you want it. The important thing is just *not to eat any food.*"

I nodded solemnly. How could anyone think a program that told you not to eat *anything* could be good for you? "How long do we do this?"

"Seven days," Piper said. "By pageant day, we'll be all slimmed down and gorgeous." She smiled kindly. "And if you improve in *every* other area, you might have a shot at the crown."

Fallon snorted.

"Yeah, *maybe,*" Deirdre mumbled, fluffing her hair.

Before I could say anything else, my cell phone rang. Saved by the bell, I thought, placing the jar on my table and smiling at Piper. "I'd better take this. See you tomorrow."

Piper nodded and she, Deirdre, and Fallon took off as I held the phone to my ear and pressed Talk. "Hello?"

"You took my case, didn't you?"

It was Portia. "Of course I did, Portia," I replied, wondering what her sharp tone was about. I'd called her as soon as I got home from our trip to Fleur and explained that I had agreed there was something fishy about her dethroning.

"Then why haven't you called me since?" Portia demanded. I could hear her pacing, high-heeled footsteps back and forth. "Ned told me you knew what you were doing. I expected updates—some idea of how it's going."

"It's going well," I replied. "I'm competing in the pageant, and—"

"Wait. What? *You?*" Portia laughed an uncharitable laugh.

I took a deep breath. "Yes, me," I replied. "Actually, this is kind of a bad time for me. Why don't we meet this afternoon?"

Sadly, it looked like I was going to have to part with my afternoon nap. Oh, well. I'm sure Piper would tell me I needed the exercise, anyway.

When I spotted Portia sitting tensely at a metal table in the courtyard of the university student center, drumming her fingers on the tabletop, I felt a rush of dread. Don't let her intimidate you, Nancy, I told myself. You're making good headway on this case.

"Hi!" I said brightly, trying to channel my inner pageant queen as I sat down across from Portia. "It's good to see you again, Portia. It's about time that we caught up."

Portia looked unconvinced. "Do you have news?" she asked bluntly. "It's been days since we last spoke."

"I do, actually." I leaned forward. "Like I told you, I decided to compete in the pageant this year so I can get an idea of who the players are."

"And . . . how's that going for you?" Her expression implied that she thought I must've been chewed up and spat out already by the whole experience—or maybe Cupcake, specifically.

"It's going well," I said lightly, not wanting to elaborate. "The good news is, I have some leads."

Portia's eyes widened. "And?" she asked eagerly.

I took a breath. "It seems to me, Portia, that the benefits of being Miss Pretty Face are pretty amazing."

"They are," she agreed. "And when someone takes them away, you miss them."

I leaned in. "To me, that means that the person who had the most to gain from your dethroning is the person who was going to take your place."

"Uh-huh." Portia nodded impatiently.

I sighed. "Portia, I've done some research, and it seems to me that Kelly McMahon had the most to gain from setting you up." A rush of guilt came over me, and I quickly added, "I'm not saying that Kelly's behind it. It's possible she doesn't even know about it. But she, or her father, Kyle, seem like the most likely suspects to me."

I leaned back, crossing my arms uncomfortably. It felt strange to be talking about Kelly like this, even though I knew she had the most to gain from Portia's dethroning.

Portia was watching me with a slightly annoyed expression. Her lack of excitement seemed strange—especially since *she* was the one who had called me looking for leads.

"That would make sense, Nancy," Portia said

evenly, "if Kelly had been the runner-up."

What? I uncrossed my arms, leaning in again. "What do you mean? You were dethroned, and she got the crown. I assumed . . ."

Portia shook her head, sighing. "Kelly wasn't the runner-up," she told me. "She was Miss Congeniality. But when the whole judge thing happened and they reconfigured everyone's scores, she was next in line and she became the runner-up."

Judge thing? Reconfigured everyone's scores? "Wait a minute, wait a minute," I said, "what judge thing? Why were the scores reconfigured?"

Portia frowned, looking at me like she couldn't believe I didn't know this. "Last year, right after I was dethroned, one of the judges came forward. She said she had scored us unfairly to favor one contestant—who happened to be the runner-up. I don't remember the details, but it was something to do with the contestant's background: She knew the family, they were struggling with money, so she wanted this girl to get the scholarship. But after my so-called 'scandal,' she had a crisis of conscience and came forward."

I didn't know what to say. I'd thought I was making headway on this case, but apparently I'd been missing some pretty important information.

Who knew there was so much intrigue behind the sparkly crowns and sashes?

"Wow," I said finally. "I guess my theory is off, then. Portia, I wish you'd told me this earlier."

Portia shrugged, not looking one bit apologetic. "You took the case," she said. "Ned said you were this crack detective. I thought you'd figure it out." With that, she reached into her bag and pulled out a mirror and some lip gloss. She applied a perfect berry-colored pout and smacked her lips, releasing the scent of strawberry into the air.

"All right," I said finally. Portia hadn't given me the whole story, but it never pays to get mad at the people you're helping. It just means they'll be less comfortable giving you the information you need. "So the runner-up wasn't Kelly; that pretty much means she had no motive. Scratch my original theory. So who *was* the runner-up?"

Portia shrugged again, dabbing at the edges of her lips with her finger. "Some girl named Robin Depken."

Depken. My stomach gave a jolt. Was it possible my Master Cleanse partner could be behind Portia's dethroning? "Do you mean Piper Depken?"

Portia shook her head, looking at me with

that same "I can't believe you don't know this already" expression. "I mean *Robin*. Piper's her sister. And if you want to talk to her, she works over at the Seaver Hall cafeteria."

RUNNER-UP

"**W**ell, well, well," a girl with soft, light blond hair pinned up in a hairnet greeted me and Portia as we approached her at the taco station. "There she *was,* Miss America."

"I could say the same to you," Portia hissed.

Portia had told me on the way over to the cafeteria that she and Robin weren't friends, that Robin wasn't her "type." I wasn't sure what she meant by that, but I hoped interviewing Robin would answer that and several other questions.

Robin shrugged. "The difference is, I was innocent. I had nothing to do with that judge's scoring issues. They disqualified me because they didn't know what else to do." She looked Portia in the eye, a grin spreading across her face. "You, on the other hand, decided the world owed you some free dresses. And you were dethroned for stealing."

Portia glared. "I didn't steal anything. I told you that before. Anyway, I'm not here just for the pleasure of your company." She stepped back and gestured to me. Robin glanced over at me with a mildly curious expression. "This is——"

"Sarah," I cut in, throwing Portia a meaningful glance. All I needed was to have my cover blown to the sister of another contestant!

"Whatever," Portia said, examining her manicure. "*Sarah* is investigating my dethroning, and she wanted to talk to you." She leaned closer to Robin and lowered her voice. "It seems that the runner-up had the most to gain from getting me dethroned. But you wouldn't know anything about that, would you?"

Robin turned to me with a horrified expression. Over the years I think I've gotten pretty good at reading faces, and hers, to me, had a look of total horrified surprise. It *didn't* seem like the guilty look of a person who knows she's done something and is finally being caught. But I put aside this information; I wasn't ready to count her out as a suspect.

"Hi," I said. "Listen, Portia, why don't you wait for me in the dining room. I'd like to talk to Robin alone."

Portia didn't look happy, but she stalked off toward the dining room. Robin looked up at me warily.

"Is it true?" she asked. "You're investigating Portia's dethroning?"

I nodded. "She asked me to look into it, and it *does* seem like there are some suspicious elements to the official story."

Robin sighed, looking at the floor. "Portia *would* go down fighting. She wouldn't take *hers* lying down."

"Hers what?" I asked.

Robin looked up and shrugged, like it was obvious. "We were both victims of a scandal. We both lost out on scholarship money. But I don't really have the . . . *resources* . . . to hire a detective."

I nodded. "Well, I'd be happy to tell you what I learn. What do you know about the scoring issue?"

Robin scowled. "That it was a lot of crap, just like everything else involving that pageant."

"What do you mean?"

Robin looked concerned for a minute, like

she hadn't meant to let that slip out. Then she sighed and shook her head. "All of it," she said. "You don't know what it's like. The way they push those stupid cosmetics, and all the politics, and *everything*."

I didn't like the sound of this. "Politics?"

Robin looked up at me. "That pageant is the biggest joke. The real competition has nothing to do with the contestants."

A chill went down my spine. For some reason, the intensity of Robin's voice was really getting to me. "Isn't your sister competing this year?" I asked.

Robin nodded. "Yeah. But only because her friend Fallon convinced her it would be fun. I would have put a stop to it, but if by some crazy chance she *won* and got the scholarship . . ." She sighed, running a rag over the counter between the food trays. "Then she wouldn't have to work two jobs to pay for school, like me. But I hate that pageant, and those cosmetics are—I wouldn't even put them on my skin. I won't let Piper, either, outside the pageant."

I frowned. Robin had reason to be bitter, I guessed, but for some reason the strength of her bitterness surprised me. "What's wrong with Pretty Face?"

Robin bit her lip, then seemed to regain her composure. "Isn't it obvious? Pretty Face hasn't been very good to me."

"So you're saying you didn't even know the judge who said she skewed the vote in your favor?"

Robin shook her head. "That's what's so stupid. I guess she used to play cards with my mother. But I didn't know her. I certainly didn't put her up to it."

I nodded. "What about Portia?"

Robin looked up at me, her eyes wide with surprise. "You seriously think I might have set her up?" she asked.

I hesitated. "I didn't say that," I insisted. "But you have to admit . . . you have a stronger motive than anyone. You needed the scholarship money. You didn't know you would be disqualified. . . ."

Robin opened her mouth and laughed a mirthless, stunned laugh. "And how would I *do* it?" she asked. "Call up my powerful business associates? Bribe them with tacos?" She gestured to the taco bar in front of her. "Look, Sarah, I guess I should be flattered that you think I'm this criminal mastermind. But the truth is, I have no money and no connections. And *no*, I didn't like Portia, and when her name was called, I wished like crazy that they were calling mine instead."

She shrugged. "But I *swear* to you, Sarah, I had nothing to do with her dethroning."

I sighed, looking away from Robin's intense gaze. The truth was, I believed her. And that left me without any leads, with a week of pageant rehearsals still ahead of me, and Portia in the next room, ready to draw my blood.

"Thanks, Robin," I said, flashing a sincere smile. "I appreciate your talking to me. I'll let you know if I have any more questions."

I walked out of the cafeteria and into the dining hall, feeling Robin's eyes on me the whole way.

"So?" Portia asked, twirling a lock of hair around her finger as she leaned against the wall.

I sighed. "I don't think she had anything to do with your dethroning."

Portia nodded slowly. "Yeah. I'd be surprised if Robin had anything to do with it."

"Why?" I asked.

Portia shrugged. "Her family just doesn't have a lot of power," she replied simply.

She turned on her heel, and I followed her out of the dining hall.

Since we'd walked from the student center all the way to Seaver Hall, I had a long, windy walk to get back to my SUV. The dinner hour was over, and darkness was falling over the campus. I said good-bye to Portia and headed off along the quiet, wooded pathway to the parking lot.

I was feeling really frustrated. I'd given so much to this case, even *joining a pageant*, and I still had nothing. Nothing except a jar of mysterious murky liquid and an increasingly dim view of pageants. I tried to run all the suspects through my head as my footsteps echoed off the pathway: Kelly? Kyle? Robin? Cupcake, maybe? No, that didn't seem likely. Fallon? No, she'd dropped out of competition last year. Unless there was someone else . . . someone I hadn't even come into contact with . . . how was I ever going to solve this case?

Thunk. A sudden noise came from behind me, and my whole body stiffened. I hadn't heard anyone back there. Was someone trying to sneak up on me?

I whirled around, searching the woods and trying to hide the fact that I was shaking like a leaf. There was no one there. But all of my senses were on alert. Still trembling, I turned back around and walked quickly toward the parking lot.

A few minutes later, I heard a *snap*, like a

branch breaking underneath someone's foot. I turned again, searching the murky darkness of the woods. Could someone be sneaking behind me on the path, then darting into the woods? Adrenaline rushed through me, and I could feel my hands shaking. Why would anyone follow me? Maybe there was a culprit behind Portia's dethroning who I hadn't discovered yet—a *dangerous* culprit, who wanted to keep me from finding out the truth.

Even as shaken as I was, I had to admit that there didn't seem to be anyone behind me. Maybe the sounds I heard were squirrels, or other animals just going about their routine business in the woods. Still, I quickened my pace again. Just as I was about to reach the parking lot, I heard another sound. It was hard to describe, like a whisper, or the sound of a winter parka brushing up against itself. It was a very *human* sound, and made me feel like ice was running through my veins.

Thinking fast, I reached into my bag and grabbed my cell phone. I punched in a random series of digits, sweeping the woods again with my eyes. "Hi there," I said loudly, trying to sound casual as the dial tone echoed in my ear. "I just wanted to let you know I'm running a little late. In fact, *right now* I'm still on the university campus. Yeah, you know that path from Seaver Hall to the visitor parking lot? I'm right near the lot. I shouldn't be too much longer."

The echo of my voice faded into the night and there was no sound except crickets and the faint sound of cars driving by on the nearby highway. I took a breath, my mind reeling. Maybe my little show had all been for nothing; maybe no one was following me at all. After all, it was dark, and I'd been keyed up ever since I'd heard that *thunk*. Was it possible that I was imagining this whole thing?

"Hey!" The sound startled me so much that I jumped, not realizing until a few seconds later that the voice was familiar. "I think I know that beautiful hair and that blue sweater! Now just turn around, and I'll know for sure when I see your blue eyes . . ."

"Ned!" I cried, cramming my cell phone back into my purse as he walked toward me from an adjoining path. I ran toward him, flushed with relief. "I'm so glad it's you!"

"I'm glad to see you too, Nancy," Ned replied, leaning in to give me a quick hug. "Portia said she had a meeting with you. I hope she's not turning into too much trouble."

I laughed, then shook my head. "She's definitely a handful, but for some crazy reason, I'm enjoying the case." I swallowed. "Even though I have no leads. And I'm beginning to hate beauty pageants."

Ned just grinned. "Nance, you'll always be Miss Pretty Face to me."

I chuckled. "Good. Remind me of that after the pageant, when I've come in last place."

We chatted some more as Ned took my hand and escorted me back to my car. He told me about a history paper he was writing about the Vietnam War, and I told him what I'd learned about the Miss Pretty Face pageant.

"Wow," Ned said. "I had no idea all these scandals were going on. I thought pageants were just about pretty girls wearing evening gowns."

"I guess nothing's that simple, Ned." Unlocking the driver's side door and climbing in, I suddenly remembered the source of my panic just a few minutes before. "Anyway, I'm so glad you spotted me at Seaver Hall. Walking that path back to the car, I got so nervous—I thought you were some bad guy following me!" I laughed lightly, but noticed Ned's expression of concern. "What is it?" I asked.

He looked uncomfortable. "I didn't see you at Seaver Hall, Nance."

I shivered. "You didn't? But—you were following me on the path!" I searched Ned's face for any sign of recognition. "Right?"

Ned shook his head slowly. "I saw you from the parking lot, which is right next to my night class," he said. His eyebrows furrowed. "You thought someone was following you?"

My heart was pounding. But I was determined not to make a big deal out of nothing. I hadn't seen anyone, and the dark woods were probably playing tricks with my mind. "I thought maybe," I said carefully. "But I'm sure it was nothing. I didn't see anyone. I'm sure it was just a squirrel or something." A squirrel wearing a parka, I thought. But I bit my lip to keep from saying it.

"Are you sure?" Ned asked, squeezing my hand as I sat in my car. "You're being safe, Nancy, aren't you?"

"Of course," I replied, quickly leaning in to kiss Ned on the cheek. "You know me. You know I'm always careful. Now go back to your dorm and finish up that paper."

Ned gave me a quick peck and we said our good nights. I locked my doors and started the car, pausing to watch him walk confidently back to the main campus.

I was pretty sure I had heard someone.

Either I was wrong, or this case was a lot more dangerous than I thought.

MISJUDGED

The next morning, after a quick call to George, I mixed up a small jug of instant lemonade and dug in the pantry to find a small jar of red food coloring. Carefully, I added a drop, then two, shaking the jug so the color blended through all of the liquid. "That's just about right," I murmured to myself. "But it's still not murky enough. . . ." I looked around the pantry, quickly spotting the answer. "Confectioners' sugar!" I dumped in two heaping spoonfuls, shaking the jug just enough to evenly disperse it. "Bingo!" The liquid looked just like the "lemonade" Piper had given me, but I could drink it freely without worrying about being "cleansed" of something I really needed. I took a sip: It was a little sweet, but otherwise drinkable.

I turned and saw Dad standing behind me, holding his travel mug full of coffee. "Getting some snacks for your big day of rehearsals?" he asked with a grin. Last night, after I got home, I'd told him about the case I was working—and about the pageant.

"Something like that," I agreed. No need to tell Dad about the Master Cleanse—he already thought pageants were wonky enough. "Are you looking for your creamer?" I could hear Hannah Gruen, our housekeeper, who was really more like family, washing pots and pans in the sink, cleaning up from the amazing pancake breakfast she'd made us. No matter how grueling today's rehearsal was going to be, I knew I'd have plenty of fuel to run on.

Dad reached around me to pick up his favorite almond-flavored coffee creamer. "How's it going?" he asked, tipping some creamer into his mug. "Finding any intrigue behind the sparkles?"

I groaned. "More intrigue than I wanted. It's a crazy world behind the tiaras, Dad. But you can check me out at the pageant itself next week." I patted his shoulder. "Just don't be offended if I don't win."

Dad smiled. "You don't need a crown to impress me, Nancy. Good luck with the case."

I hugged him before stepping out of the pantry. "Thanks."

At the pageant rehearsal, Piper seemed totally fooled by my fake "lemonade." Score one for Nancy Drew. Unfortunately, that was the only thing to go my way all morning. I'd brought the dress I'd worn to a formal dance for the evening gown competition; it was simple and strapless, a satin robin's egg blue. I'd had plenty of happy memories in that dress, dancing the night away with Ned. But Cupcake seemed to think it was a monstrosity.

"*Nancy,*" she called out, for what seemed like the hundredth time. "*That* is the dress you're planning to wear? That seems like an appropriate choice to you?"

I looked around. It was our first dress rehearsal for the evening gown segment, and everyone else was dressed in flashy, spangled, bead-and-sequin numbers. Fallon wore a glittering black dress with roses beaded up the leg, and smirked at my stunned expression. Even Deirdre was dressed in a sparkly pink sheath. I wasn't sure what to say. Where had they found these crazy dresses?

"I thought this dress was flattering on me," I replied honestly.

"It would be," sniffed Cupcake, "if you were a nun. I *urge* you to reconsider." And with that, she started the rehearsal.

Humph.

"Nancy," Kelly said gently when we were back in the dressing room to change, "don't take it too hard."

"Oh, I'm not," I said honestly, then figured that was the wrong approach, since Kelly thought I was in this pageant to win it. "I mean, it *was* a little surprising, I guess. Your dress was really something else. Where did you get it?"

Kelly had worn an intricate purple, teal, and green dress that had made her look like a perfectly groomed peacock. The beadwork was beautiful.

Kelly blushed. "Oh, I didn't buy it, Nancy. I think you'll find that very few of these girls actually own their evening gowns." She leaned in. "It's kind of customary to borrow your evening gown from a local store, in exchange for mentioning them at the pageant. You get the dress you need, and they get free publicity. Everybody wins!"

Hmmm. It would never have occurred to me to try to borrow such a sparkly, fancy dress, but actually I *could* use some face time with the local boutiques. That gave me an idea. "Thanks for the tip, Kelly."

"Anytime." Kelly smiled, then turned back to her dressing station to put on her makeup. "By the way," she called, "I thought your dress *was* really flattering, Nancy."

Fallon, whose dressing station was near mine, rolled her eyes.

I grabbed my cell phone and dialed Bess's number. "Hey," I said, when she answered. "Are you up for a little more shopping this afternoon?"

Bess groaned as we pulled into the parking lot for Glamore—"for the woman who believes more is more!"

"Of all the boutiques in all the mini-malls in all of River Heights, why *this* one?" she asked. She'd brought her usual stash of fashion magazines with her, but when she saw where we were going, she threw them back under her seat, as though they would do her no good here.

I parked the car and unclipped my seat belt. "What's wrong with this one?" I asked.

"Nancy, *look* at this stuff." Bess gestured to the window, where an array of big-haired mannequins were posing in an assortment of jewel-encrusted gowns. "Don't you think it's kind of . . . overstated?"

I shrugged. "In the pageant world they call it *glamorous.*"

Bess laughed. "Come on. You can see these dresses from space. Why won't they let you wear your blue dress?"

I sighed. "Apparently, it's a little too plain," I replied. "For a pageant, at least. And I'm trying to *do* the whole pageant thing and take it seriously. I thought you'd be proud." I looked at Bess with just the hint of a grin.

"You're here to find out more about Portia's case," she guessed without a hitch.

"Oh, Bess," I said, opening my door and climbing out. "You know me too well."

Sabrina Balint-Duncan, the owner of Glamore, was the judge who had come forward to confess to throwing her scores of last year's contestants. George had figured this out for me that morning, via a quick Internet news search. By coming into her store as a contestant, and asking her advice on gowns and pageants in general, I was hoping to get her into a comfortable place where she might tell me more about why she'd fixed Robin's scores.

George had adamantly refused to accompany me and Bess on this particular mission. "Froofy women shopping for sparkly gowns?" she had said. "Nancy, you know I would do anything to help you solve a mystery, but . . ."

"But you'd rather be doing anything else?" I asked.

George had laughed. "But I happen to know the perfect girl for the job."

Bess and I approached Glamore's front door. I could already see tons of sparkling, flashing evening gowns. To the left of the store, a bustling salon was filled with older women, all having their hair cut or colored or permed.

"Good morning, darling," a middle-aged woman with teased auburn hair and sunset-hued eyelids greeted Bess and me as we walked in.

"Good morning," I replied. "I hope you can help me. I'm competing in this year's Miss Pretty Face pageant—"

"Ah!" cried the woman, running out from behind the sales counter. "Oh, you must tell me everything! I am Sabrina, I own Glamore! You're here for a dress, yes?"

I nodded. "An evening gown," I said. "I was told by a fellow contestant that you loan them out."

"Oh, yes, yes." Sabrina ran to my side, reaching

out to grab the waistband of my jeans, looking me up and down, hemming and hawing. "Your arms, you want to hide them. They are not toned." Ignoring Bess, she grabbed my arm and pulled me over to a rack of long, short-sleeved sequined gowns. "This cut, it is called the pageant dress. It is perfect. For you, I think, pink." She reached into the spangles and pulled out a floor-length pink-sequined dress with a sunset beach scene and—oddly—a flamingo beaded down the left leg.

"What do you think?" asked Sabrina.

"Wow," I said honestly. "Just, wow."

Sabrina nodded, pursing her lips in satisfaction. "It is right, I think. You try it on." She gestured to a small dressing area toward the rear of the store. Nodding, I took the dress from her—it weighed *at least* twenty pounds—and lugged it over to the dressing area. Bess, still standing near the entrance, gave me an enjoying-this-way-too-much thumbs-up.

Once in the dress, I looked down at myself. The sequins seemed to sparkle with the brightness of a thousand diamonds. The dress was so heavy, it made my shoulders slump, and so long that it drooped on the floor when I was in bare feet. When I wore heels, though, I knew it would fall just at the right length.

I stepped out of the dressing room.

"Ah!" cried Sabrina in delight.

"Ahhhh!" cried Bess, bringing her hands to her mouth. I could see she was trying to keep herself from laughing. And failing. I could see her shoulders heaving with giggles.

If that was Bess's reaction, I couldn't wait till George saw this dress.

As Sabrina came over to me, adjusting the dress and suggesting accessories, Bess turned away and started looking around the store. I decided to take the opportunity to try to get some information from Sabrina.

"I heard, actually," I began as Sabrina held a pair of chandelier earrings up to my ears, "that you used to judge Miss Pretty Face?"

Sabrina glanced up to meet my eyes in the mirror. Her expression was unreadable. "Yes."

"But you're not doing it this year?" I prompted.

Sabrina's eyes cut away. "No."

"Is there any reason for that?" I asked. "Did you get tired of it or just, I don't know, frustrated with the whole system?" I lowered my voice confidentially. "I want to know what I'm up against."

Sabrina looked up again, frowning into the

mirror, then sighed. "It is simple. I was asked not to judge again, because I made a mistake last time. A big mistake."

My eyes widened. It impressed me that Sabrina just came out with her scandal like that; I'd been prepared for lots of follow-up questions. "I can't imagine that," I said. "What did you do?"

Sabrina sighed again. As we spoke, she never stopped fussing with my dress or holding up new accessories. That interested me because most people have to concentrate on an upsetting conversation; they stop all other activity. If she was able to carry on with the dress fitting, it seemed like the pageant scandal wasn't that upsetting to her; maybe she'd made peace with it.

"I play cards with this woman. When we play, she talks about her daughters. How they are struggling for money, how they might not afford college. One of her daughters was a contestant. She was likable, bubbly. I wanted her to win, for her family. But truthfully, she was not the best Miss Pretty Face."

Sabrina paused and met my eyes in the mirror. "I gave her the best scores, anyway. It was wrong of me. I told myself I was doing something nice for the family, but it was wrong. She didn't win, and I told myself it was over, no big deal. But then the scandal happened. With the other girl, you know. And she was dethroned, and this other girl was about to become Miss Pretty Face—because of my scores. The scores which had nothing to do with whether or not she would make the right Miss Pretty Face."

She shook her head. "I could not live with it. I called the pageant. They disqualified this girl and recalculated the scores. Now, another girl is Miss Pretty Face. And I am not invited back."

I nodded slowly. "Wow," I said. She had described Robin as "bubbly"—something I had trouble imagining, but maybe it was true, back then. Nothing about Sabrina's manner made me think that she was lying.

"I feel awful about the girl who was disqualified because of me," she told me. "But I felt I couldn't let her win just because I lied. And I thought better of the other girls in the competition. I feel for all of them." She paused, stepping back from the mirror and smiling at my spangled, sparkly reflection. "Now I only give dresses to pageant girls."

I looked in the mirror. The dress reflected a thousand little glimmers of light, and glittery rhinestones dangled from my wrist and ears. I didn't exactly look *classy*. But, I had to admit, I sort of lit up the room.

"Thanks," I told Sabrina.

"How'd it go?" Bess asked when I returned to her with my borrowed dress and jewelry. She'd long since lost interest in the glittery clothing and had positioned herself near the door.

"Okay, I guess," I whispered. "I think she's telling the truth. Unfortunately."

Bess looked curious. "Why unfortunately?"

"Because that leaves me with no leads at all," I replied with a sigh. "Again."

"I wouldn't be so sure about that. Look." Bess pointed to a small framed picture that hung on the wall. It was a photo of the River Heights High School Girls' Cross-Country Team, signed by all the girls "with thanks to Glamore for being our sponsor." I squinted at the faces in the photo. One stood out: a grinning, pink-cheeked Fallon Gregory.

"Okay," I replied. "So Fallon Gregory runs cross-country."

"Yes, but apparently she ran last year." Bess paused, waiting for me to catch up. "Didn't you say she dropped out of the pageant last year because she had mono?"

I thought for a second. Then it hit me! "And cross-country starts up at the same time of year as the pageant! Bess, you're a genius! How could she have run cross-country with mono?"

Bess just grinned happily. "So I guess this wasn't a wasted trip."

My mind was spinning with this new information. "I guess not," I agreed, squeezing her arm gratefully. "Thanks to you!"

8

LIAR LIAR

It's true, Fallon lying about why she'd dropped out of last year's pageant didn't seem to *directly* relate to Portia's dethroning. Still, if she had lied about this one point, who knew what else she was lying about? I was determined to get to the bottom of this. And, fortunately, I was pretty sure I had an in to the girls' cross-country team.

"Hi, Emily!" I greeted a petite, dark-haired library assistant in the children's section of the River Heights Public Library a couple days later. "Remember me?" Emily and I weren't close friends, but we've known each other a long time, and she's helped me with library research before.

"Of course, Nancy!" she replied with a smile. "What'll it be this time? Traffic laws in Milan?

The freezing point of Elmer's glue?"

I laughed. "Nothing that involved, this time." I leaned over the checkout counter. "I have a question for you. Did you run cross-country with the River Heights team last year?"

Emily looked a little surprised, but she nodded. "Sure," she said. "I ran with them every year."

"Did you have a teammate named Fallon Gregory?"

Emily's eyes sparkled with recognition. "Sure," she replied. "Fallon. She had kind of an attitude sometimes, but boy, could she run!"

"And she ran last year?" I asked.

Emily nodded. "Sure," she replied. "She was a great competitor."

"No health problems?" I pressed.

Emily wrinkled her nose, thinking. "Not that I could tell," she replied finally. "She acted perfectly healthy. And she had a great season."

I nodded slowly. "So you never heard of her having mono?"

Emily looked surprised. "Mono?" she asked. "That's pretty debilitating, isn't it? And it can last for months?"

I nodded. "It causes extreme fatigue. It would be almost impossible to compete in a sport."

Emily frowned. "No, there's no way," she said

finally. "But she did miss a bunch of school earlier that year, like three weeks, in February. I think she said her aunt died. But maybe it was mono?"

Hmmmm. Now *that* was a long time to be absent from school. I quickly wrote that down. "Thanks, Emily," I said, looking up with a smile. "You've been a big help."

Emily grinned, leaning back and pulling over a stack of newly returned novels. "I like to do whatever I can to aid the pursuit of justice, Nancy."

Later that evening, Bess and I were sprawled on my bed while George clicked away on her tiny laptop computer on my desk, drinking (real) lemonade and eating a plate of Hannah's amazing oatmeal-raisin cookies. I had asked George to hack into the River Heights High School attendance records, something she seemed to think would be no problem. George is *amazing* with anything electronic.

George half-smiled as she worked, biting into a cookie. "So how's the pageant going, Nancy?" she asked. "I mean, aside from the humiliation, the scandals, the backstabbing, and that horror of a dress Bess told me about."

Bess giggled into a pillow.

I sighed. "You've pretty much covered it all," I said. "Except for a bunch of other embarrassments that have taught me I was really *never* meant to be Miss *Anything*."

"Details, please," Bess sang, flouncing off the bed to steal a cookie off George's plate.

"Well, let's see, there was the time I stepped on Deirdre's foot during dance rehearsal," I counted off with my fingers, "and the time I forgot my own name during interview rehearsals. And then, during my talent rehearsal, Cupcake pointed out that I seemed to have discovered a note only animals could hear."

"Ouch," George responded, biting her lip to keep from laughing. "Maybe we should have sent Bess undercover."

I threw my pillow at George. "Don't get smart with me," I joked. "Or on my next beauty pageant case, I'm sending *you* undercover."

"That," Bess said, shoving the rest of the cookie in her mouth, "is something that I would love to see."

George chuckled, then her face brightened as she brought up an Excel document. "I think I'm in!" she said cheerfully. "This looks like the attendance records, and if I just search for 'Gregory' . . ."

Bess and I leaned over her shoulder. "Fallon was absent in February," I reminded George.

George continued scrolling down, then over. "Bingo!" she said, gesturing to a line on the screen. There they were—a whole string of bright red A's for "absent," lined up with Fallon Gregory's name.

"So she *was* out of school then," I murmured, counting the A's with my finger. "For . . . twelve school days! That's almost three weeks."

George nodded. "That's a really long time."

"Maybe her aunt really *did* die," Bess murmured.

"I guess," I said. "It just seems so coincidental. Between that, and her dropping out last year, and lying about mono . . . I feel like there's something right in front of me and I just can't see it."

George started clicking around in the River Heights High School database. "Here—student records," she said. Scrolling down, she located "Gregory, Fallon," and clicked on the link.

"Ugh!" Bess cried in horror as a full-page photo came up on-screen. "Who knew they keep your freshman picture on file *forever*? I'm pretty sure Fallon wouldn't want *anyone* to remember her this way."

I looked at the screen. Sure enough, poor

freshman Fallon stared back awkwardly. Clunky square glasses hid her pretty blue eyes, and her hair frizzed in an unflattering poofy cut around her ears. She looked like an entirely different person. In fact . . . was that even Fallon? I leaned closer, gently pushing George aside and taking the laptop in my own hands for a closer look. No, it was Fallon—those sparkly eyes didn't lie. But even beyond the frizzy hair and thick glasses . . .

"It's strange," I said. "I know it's her. But there's something *different* about her, something I can't put my finger on."

"Hmmm." George examined the photo with me, then motioned for me to give the laptop back so she could do some more searching. After clicking around for another couple minutes, George's face lit up. "There," she said, her eyes moving back and forth, I assumed between two different photos. Smiling, she handed the laptop to me. "Which of these things is not like the other?" she sang.

I looked at the screen as Bess looked on over my shoulder. On the left was a photo George had located of the Fallon *I* knew: gorgeous, blond, decked out in a sequined silver dress. It was probably a prom photo. On the right, poor freshman Fallon looked like she wanted to sink into the background. I looked back and forth, comparing. Back and forth . . .

"Her nose!" I cried, pointing to freshman Fallon's nose, which, as Dad would say, had "character." It was slightly crooked and pointed down at her pretty-but-shy smile. In the other photo Fallon's nose had been whittled down to the cute-as-a-button nose *I* knew: dainty, straight, with a tiny upturn at the end. It actually reminded me of the nose of one of Bess's favorite starlets.

Bess nodded. "Getting a nose job, between the surgery itself and recovery, can take a long time."

"Like . . . three weeks, depending on where you got it done and how much damage they had to do?" George asked.

"They did a beautiful job," Bess observed. "She looks great, but it's subtle. Which is probably why no one at school noticed."

I nodded. The gears in my brain were already whirring. Quickly, I grabbed my cell phone and dialed Kelly's number.

"What are you doing?" George asked, but I held up my finger for her to give me a minute.

"Hey, Nancy," Kelly greeted me, pausing to take a slurpy sip of something. "I know it sounds like I'm being bad right now, but I promise you, it's an all-fruit smoothie. What's up?"

I cringed. It would be really great to be done with his pageant and get away from an atmosphere where drinking a milk shake made you "bad." "Not much," I lied. "I'm just recovering from that workout Cupcake assigned us for homework."

Kelly groaned. "I *know,*" she replied. "Isn't it awful? I didn't think I'd get through it."

I laughed, trying to sound light. "I've decided I'm not doing anymore," I told Kelly. "Tomorrow, I'm scheduling an appointment for lipo! It sounds much easier, doesn't it?"

Kelly laughed, but as she recovered, she sounded more serious. "Now, Nancy," she cautioned. "You can't do that. You know plastic surgery is grounds for disqualification. And you don't want to mess up when you've come this far!"

I forced a chuckle. Just as I thought. "Okay, okay," I said. "Oh, listen—I have to go. My dad just got home. Enjoy your smoothie."

"See you tomorrow, Nancy."

I clicked the End button and slowly turned back to George.

"So?" Bess asked. "What was that about?"

Bess raised an eyebrow at me "*Lipo,* Nancy?"

I shook my head. "I just made that up to bring up the topic," I explained. "And it seems my hunch was right. Plastic surgery is grounds for disqualification from the Miss Pretty Face pageant."

George's eyes widened. "But Fallon's competing now."

"That's because no one knows," I explained, thinking it over. "Or actually, *someone* knows. The same someone who found out about it last year, and used that information to blackmail her into dropping out of the pageant." I chewed my lip, still thinking. "It must have been part of their deal that she could compete this year. So whoever blackmailed her . . . probably isn't one of this year's contestants."

Bess looked stunned. "*Wow,*" she said. "I knew pageant girls could be nasty sometimes, but *wow*. That is really underhanded."

"It sure is," I agreed. "And I'd better find out who's behind it. Because he or she might be behind some *other* underhanded schemes—like getting Portia dethroned."

A RELATIVE SURPRISE

With my twenty-pound sparkling pink pageant dress draped over me, I held my shoulders high, straightened my shoulders, and pasted a blinding smile across my face. One, two, one, two, I counted off, timing my steps to beats in the music. I could see Kelly winking and giving me the thumbs-up from her spot at the front of the stage, but I didn't break my concentration. Trying to move swiftly and elegantly, I stepped up onto the tiny platform I was assigned for the evening gown number, and waved a slow, deliberate, pageant wave.

"*Nancy!*" cried Cupcake, as she had pretty much every time I'd graced the stage in every rehearsal. I was so used to it, I didn't even tense up anymore. I just looked at her eagerly, waiting to hear her criticism.

"That was *beautiful!*" Cupcake beamed, looking as satisfied as if she'd just run the Boston Marathon. It took me a minute to register what she'd said. *Beautiful?* Wait, I did well?

"Thank you!" I cried, a wave of pride running through me. Finally!

"I'm so proud of you," Cupcake continued, after moving her attention to all of us contestants. "You are twelve beautiful, elegant, and accomplished young women. For the first time, I think you're all worthy of a reign as Miss Pretty Face."

All of my competitors burst into smiles, and there was a smattering of polite applause. I couldn't believe it—but for the first time I actually *felt* like a pageant girl. Not that I'd be rushing out to compete in more pageants as soon as this one ended. But for the first time, I saw the appeal. After all of our rehearsals, I did feel more poised, more confident—more beautiful.

Back at my dressing station, I wiped my makeup off with cold cream and carefully capped, covered, and put away all of the Pretty Face Cosmetics I'd been using. Immediately, I looked less glamorous—but it was almost a relief.

Perfect Face, that "revitalizer" we were supposed to wear all the time, did make my face glow, but also left a funny tingle. When I wore it, my face felt tighter—something I guessed some girls might be looking for, but not me.

I quickly changed into jeans and a sweater, zipping my loaner pageant dress back into its garment bag and hoisting it over my shoulder. I'd left other outfits at my dressing station, but since the dress was very valuable (all that beadwork was expensive) and not mine, I kept it with me at all times.

"Nancy!" Kelly called, running up to me in the parking lot as I headed for my SUV. "You were *amazing* today. Really. You've improved so much!"

I realized Kelly was acknowledging that I'd been terrible before, but it didn't bother me, coming from her. "Thanks," I said sincerely. "You, on the other hand, have been amazing from day one. Are you going to keep competing in pageants once your reign ends?"

Kelly wrinkled her nose and shrugged. "I dunno," she admitted. "I mean, this is the first one I entered and I kinda lucked into the crown." She laughed. "Why mess up that winning streak?"

I chuckled, but then stopped abruptly when

I noticed someone standing by my car. A creepy feeling washed over me, remembering those sounds in the woods when I'd visited the university the other night. But when I shifted to get a better look, I realized: It was my new buddy, Portia. And once again, she didn't look happy. I groaned inwardly.

"Kelly, I think I have to go," I said, apologetic. "It looks like someone's waiting for me. See you tomorrow."

Kelly nodded. "See you tomorrow." But she followed my gaze over to my car, and her expression upon seeing Portia was not a happy one. Looking like she wanted to say something else, she shook her head and headed to her own car.

"Hello, Portia," I said as I walked up to my car, fetching my keys from my purse and moving to hang the dress in the back window.

Portia frowned at me. "I see you've got a new dress. Look at you," she observed, not warmly. "You're quite the little pageant girl now."

I opened the back door and hung the dress firmly on a hook. "When in Rome," I said.

Portia's eyes narrowed. "Maybe that's why you haven't been in touch lately, huh? Maybe you've been too busy chasing the crown to remember why you're competing in the first place."

I moved closer. "Portia, please keep your voice down," I cautioned. "The girls I'm competing with think I'm just another contestant. I see you're angry." I paused. "The truth is, I do have some new leads. But let's go somewhere else to discuss it."

Portia nodded thoughtfully. "Okay. How about you treat me to lunch to make up for it?"

I sighed, thinking of the few bills I had in my wallet. "Sounds great," I agreed, opening my door and swinging into the driver's seat. "Hope you like burgers."

A few minutes later Portia and I were seated outside the Burger Shack—me with a cheeseburger, and her with a small garden salad.

"I didn't even know they had salad here," I murmured.

Portia rolled her eyes at me. "Nancy, if you ask nicely and bat your eyelashes a lot," she said, "you can usually get what you want."

"Listen," I said, pausing to sip my soda. "I'm still not sure how this relates to your dethroning, but I've learned something interesting about Fallon Gregory."

Portia's eyes lit up at the news of fresh gossip. "You did? What?"

I paused, wanting her to take this seriously. "Actually, I think she was being blackmailed." I paused, waiting for a reaction, but Portia's face didn't change, so I continued. "She didn't drop out of the competition because she had mono. I think she dropped out because someone found out she'd had plastic surgery and was threatening to tell the judges."

I watched Portia carefully, expecting her to look pleased. I knew I hadn't solved her case yet, but this was some pretty complicated info I'd put together. But she didn't look pleased at all. If anything, she looked annoyed.

"*Fallon* was blackmailed?" she asked. "*Fallon* had to drop out of the competition? Nancy, I lost my crown and my scholarship! I may not be able to come back to school next semester! I was *humiliated* in front of the whole town!"

I leaned in, trying to put on my most soothing voice. "I know, Portia," I said, reaching out to touch her arm. "I'm not saying what she went through compares to what *you* went through."

"You can say that again," Portia scoffed.

I took a breath. "I just think that if Fallon lied about the reason she dropped out last year . . . maybe there are other things she's lying about." Portia seemed to be thinking this over. "I just think . . . if lies and deception were part of last year's competition, before you even won, then it's possible those lies could lead me to the person behind your dethroning."

Portia sighed and stuck her plastic fork in her salad, as though she were too distraught to eat any more. She seemed to be considering what I was saying, but she didn't look at all happy.

Finally her eyes turned back to me. And they were shooting daggers. "*Fine,*" she said, the word coming out sharp and angry. "I really thought, Nancy, when I hired you that you would solve my case. Ned was so nice and he talked you up so much, I had total faith in what you were doing. *Now,* though . . ." She sighed again and shook her head. "Your theory about Kelly was total bunk. And now you're researching some random lie a ridiculous girl told that's *totally* unrelated to my problem."

I cleared my throat. "*I* don't think it's totally unrelated."

Portia shook her head again. "Fine," she said, pushing back her chair and standing up. Standing, she slipped her sunglasses over her eyes and glared down at me. "Go solve *Fallon's* problem, if you want to. Maybe someday you'll get back on my case. If and when that happens, give me a call."

"Wait," I called, reaching out to grab Portia's arm. She stopped short and jerked her arm away, like my hands were made of fire.

"What?" she demanded.

I looked up at Portia. I had no idea how I'd gotten myself into this mess, but I wasn't giving up until I knew everything about this pageant that there was to know. If that made Portia unhappy, tough—she'd be a lot happier when this information helped me solve her case.

"Do you have any idea who might have black-mailed Fallon?" I asked. "Someone who was close to her, who had means to find out about the surgery."

Portia frowned, then her lips curved into a mean smile. "Why don't you ask your new *friend* Kelly?" she asked, digging in her purse for her keys. "Kelly and Fallon are cousins. And their parents are close."

With that, she turned on her heel and stalked back to her car.

I was left dumbfounded.

10

BLACKMAILED

"We're almost at the end now," Kyle McMahon told us at pageant rehearsal the next day. This time, we had dress-rehearsed the entire pageant, ending with the "talent" competition, and we were all still lined up on the stage in our costumes. For my performance of "On My Own," I wore a tattered black dress and smeared a little eyeliner on my face to look like dirt (Cupcake's idea). And lately it seemed, if my singing wasn't exactly *good,* at least it was getting a reaction.

"This is our last rehearsal, and I'm so proud of all you beautiful young ladies," Kyle went on. He glanced at Kelly, who once again was standing in front (as the reigning Miss Pretty Face, she was always supposed to be in front), and his face broke into a proud smile. She smiled back, showing her dimples. "You've clearly improved by leaps and bounds since I last I watched you rehearse, back at the beginning. I truly can't think of a better group of young ladies to represent our new Perfect Face Moisturizer and Face Revitalizer to River Heights. You all embody everything our company stands for: inner beauty, freshness, and poise. I can't imagine anyone sitting in the audience Saturday night and *not* wanting to do everything she can to look as gorgeous as all of you."

We all applauded politely. I caught Fallon's eye—she was dressed in a pink floaty ballet costume for *her* talent performance—and she scowled at me.

Don't take it personally, Nancy, I told myself. She's been through a lot in this competition.

With Kyle's speech, the rehearsal ended and we were free to change back into our street clothes and head out. After scrubbing my face (I still couldn't get used to that tingly Perfect Face), I changed into khaki pants and a peasant blouse and headed over to Kelly's dressing area.

"Nancy!" Piper stopped me, grabbing my arm as I passed by her station. Next to her, Deirdre gave me a tight smile as she reapplied a coat of crimson lip gloss. Fallon was on Piper's other side, but seemed totally involved in applying perfume. In fact, it seemed like the better I got as a beauty contestant, the cooler Fallon behaved.

"Hi, Piper," I greeted her. Piper had improved a lot during the rehearsal period too. She seemed to have improved her posture and she no longer fidgeted or seemed nervous onstage. She didn't have Fallon's impeccable Ice Princess style, but she was adorable and enthusiastic.

"Girl, I just wanted to tell you how great you look," Piper told me, gesturing to the bottle of "lemonade" in my tote bag. I'd gotten so used to carrying it around and occasionally taking a swig, I'd completely forgotten that Piper still thought I was fasting with her.

"Um—thanks," I replied, looking down at myself.

"How much weight have you lost?" Piper asked eagerly. Beside her, Deirdre turned in my direction with a raised eyebrow.

"Um," I replied, trying to think. I'd weighed myself on our bathroom scale the morning before, and I weighed the same as I always did— precisely the same I'd weighed when we'd started rehearsals. Whatever improvements Piper was seeing, they were totally in her own head. "Four pounds," I lied.

"Um," Deirdre murmured, eyeing me skeptically. "Are you sure?"

"*Wow!*" Piper cried and squeezed my arm. "Congrats! I lost six."

"You look great," I replied, realizing that she was expecting it. Piper *did* look great these days—but it had more to do with posture and styling than not eating.

Piper grinned. "I'm so glad you did this with me," she replied. "You were a little tubby before. And you totally didn't look like a beauty queen. Now you have a chance."

Now Deirdre was stifling a laugh. I forced a smile. "Thanks."

Piper squeezed my arm again and walked away with Deirdre trailing behind.

Wow, I thought dazedly as I walked over to Kelly's station. Piper's really something else.

"Hey!" I called cheerfully, approaching from behind as Kelly applied new lip gloss in her mirror. "Want to grab lunch to celebrate the end of rehearsals?"

Kelly caught my eye in the mirror and smiled warmly, but then seemed to hesitate. "I'd love to," she said, "but Nancy, before we go, I have to tell you something. You know I think you're great, right? And I really hate to judge anyone or tell them what to do."

My stomach dropped. Had Kelly found out why I was really competing in the pageant? Did she know that I was looking at her as a suspect?

Kelly turned and put her hands on my arms, looking up at me seriously. "I saw you talking to Portia Leoni in the parking lot yesterday afternoon," she said in a low voice. "Nancy, I know we haven't been friends long and I have no right to tell you who to be friends with. But I *really* think . . ." She looked around, as if she was worried that someone might be eavesdropping. "I think she's bad news."

I tilted my head. "How so?"

Portia had been dethroned in a public controversy, and most people in River Heights probably thought she was a shoplifter. But something about the urgency in Kelly's tone made me think this was more personal.

Kelly sighed, glancing up at me. "Of course you know she was dethroned," she said, not looking me in the eye. "But even before that, my dad thought she was trouble. She would stay out late, then show up late to scheduled events. She would be rude to event sponsors. Or she would ask to keep the clothes and jewelry she was loaned for promotional events." She paused, meeting my eye. "None of it was punishable, enough to threaten the crown. It was just her attitude. It started when we were competing, but it got bad once she won." Kelly bit her lip, then continued. "She always acted like she was *entitled* to something," she said. "Like the world owed her. Like everyone else was there to serve her. You know?"

Oh, I know, I thought ruefully. I wondered what Kelly would think if she knew the truth, that I had been hired by Portia to investigate her dethroning and was having to deal with her on a regular basis. I nodded, thinking. Everything Kelly said, I could see being true. I could certainly imagine that Portia hadn't been the sweetest and cuddliest Miss Pretty Face of all time. Still, I had a strange feeling that Kelly wasn't telling me everything.

"I really barely know her," I told Kelly. "She's a classmate of my boyfriend, Ned. She was in the neighborhood shopping yesterday, recognized me, and asked to borrow my phone." I shrugged.

Kelly smiled. "Oh, Nancy, I know this makes me sound like the hugest dork, but that's such a relief." She picked up her purse and slung it over her shoulder, moving closer. "I knew you were too nice to be friends with someone like her. I just saw you together, and—I don't know—I was afraid she'd corrupted you or something."

I shook my head. "I am one hundred percent uncorrupted."

Kelly smiled wider, showing all her teeth. "Tell you what. Why don't you ride home with me and Dad and we can have a private lunch at Chez McMahon?" she asked. "My dad brought home some new cosmetics the other night. We can look through my stash and see if anything suits you."

I nodded. "That sounds perfect."

Kelly linked her arm through mine, and we went off to find her father.

"How are you ladies doing?" asked Kyle for the third time an hour or so later, appearing in the dining room. "More soda for either of you? I bought fresh brownies at the bakery yesterday."

"We're fine, Dad, thanks." Kelly shot me an embarrassed look, but I waved my hand in a *don't worry about it* gesture. Truthfully, though, I found Kyle's constant supervision more than a little odd. When we'd arrived home with take-out from a local sandwich shop, Kyle had told us he was going to eat in his den—"lots of work to catch up on," he'd said, explaining, "I'm working at home today." But since then, he'd come in to check on us every ten minutes. Maybe Kelly was right, and he really was incredibly protective of his daughter. But his suffocating behavior made me wonder if he had something to hide.

"Anyway," Kelly said as I crunched on a pretzel and Kyle headed back to the kitchen, "the one thing I *will* miss when I give up the crown is the charity work. Portia chose leukemia awareness as her platform, her big issue to publicize as Miss Pretty Face, so I've spent a lot of time in hospitals, hanging out with sick kids. They're really amazing, Nancy. You'd think they would be sad or hard to talk to, but they're so sweet and bubbly and grateful for your attention." She paused to take a sip of soda. "It's made me think about becoming a doctor. I've always gotten pretty good grades in science."

"That's great," I said. "And I'm sure you can keep visiting the kids after you give up the crown. You know, unofficially."

Kelly nodded. "I definitely will. Hey, maybe you could come with me sometime, Nancy. I bet you'd like it."

"Sure, just tell me when you're going."

Kelly smiled. "I will!"

I took a sip of my soda, then leaned forward

in my chair confidentially. "So, speaking of giving up your crown," I said quietly, "who do you think will replace you?"

Kelly looked uncomfortable. "You mean . . . ?"

"Who will *win* tomorrow?" I asked with an encouraging smile. "Come on, you can tell me. And no 'It'll be you, Nancy.'"

Kelly laughed. "Oh, come on," she said. "I think it *might* be you, honestly."

I scoffed. "Stop trying to butter me up. I've improved, but I still wouldn't bet on me." Kelly shook her head uncomfortably. She was so sweet, I knew she didn't like implying in any way that I wasn't a great beauty queen—even if it was just by agreeing with me. I lowered my voice to a whisper. "Personally?" I said. "I don't think anyone has a chance of beating Fallon."

Kelly looked up, seeming relieved to be able to say something positive. "She *is* really good," she admitted. "She's been in a lot of pageants. She just has this *presence* about her."

"How was she in last year's pageant?" I asked, hoping Kelly would take the bait.

"Oh, she didn't compete last year," Kelly replied. "She dropped out because she got mono."

I nodded slowly, like I was thinking something over. "That's funny."

Kelly looked alarmed. "What?"

"I have a friend on the high school cross-country team," I replied. "She mentioned running with Fallon last year. You couldn't run with mono, could you?"

I couldn't help but notice that Kelly was beginning to look super uncomfortable. Which was good because it meant I might be getting somewhere—but bad for *me* because it meant my friend had something to hide.

She shrugged. "Can you? I don't know."

"I also thought I heard someone mention that you guys were related." Kelly looked up, then quickly away. Her expression didn't seem to deny what I was saying, but she didn't look happy to share the information, either.

"We're cousins," Kelly replied, shoving a piece of apple in her mouth.

"Are you close?" I asked.

Kelly swallowed and shrugged again. "We used to be," she said with a sigh. "Our parents still hang out a lot. But honestly, ever since we've been teenagers, Fallon doesn't . . ." She paused. "Fallon doesn't seem very interested in being close."

I nodded. "Oh."

"You see how she is," Kelly went on, shooting

me a knowing look. "She can be . . . prickly. So I kind of keep my distance."

I nodded again. "Do you know if she really had mono?" I asked.

Kelly sighed. "What does it matter?"

I paused, choosing my words carefully. "It just seems like a lot went on with the pageant last year," I said. "And I can't imagine why someone as competitive as Fallon would willingly drop out, then lie about it. I just want to know what happened, in case, you know, something comes up at *this* year's pageant."

Kelly looked down at the remains of her sandwich for a long time. Then she looked up and met my eyes. "This is the truth, Nancy," she said quietly. "I don't know why Fallon dropped out last year. And yes, it seemed really strange to me too." She paused. "Ever since she was little, Fallon wanted to be a beauty queen. We used to make our Barbie dolls compete in pageants all the time. As soon as she was old enough, Fallon started entering them. And she did pretty well. She would place second or third, but she could never win the crown." She sighed. "Then last year's Miss Pretty Face happened. She was totally gung-ho at the first two rehearsals. *So* into it, like this was the most important thing she'd ever done—like she *had* to win. And actually, I don't know what happened, but she was doing really well. It looked like she *would* win. Then suddenly . . ." She trailed off, shaking her head. "I came to rehearsal one day and she wasn't there. Cupcake told us she'd withdrawn from the competition because she had mono. I knew she didn't; I knew from her parents that she was fine and running cross-country and doing the things she always did."

"Did you confront her?" I asked.

Kelly nodded. "Like I said, we weren't close. But I was still competing in the pageant—my dad thought it would be 'good for me'"— she rolled her eyes—"so at a family dinner, I asked her privately why she'd dropped out."

I nodded. "What did she say?"

"She said to mind my own business." Kelly frowned. "She said it wasn't important, and something weird about how she had a plan, that she'd come out on top."

Hmmm. A *plan?*

"Then she added a lot of other nasty stuff about how I would never win, blah blah blah. I think she just wanted me to stop asking."

At that point, we heard footsteps approaching the dining room. Both of us looked up to see

Kyle entering, *again*—this time with a plate of brownies.

"I just couldn't resist," he said with a bright smile. "I had to have one of these for dessert. I figured you ladies would like some too."

Kelly and I smiled and thanked him. I, at least, was hoping that the less we said, the sooner he would be on his way. But unfortunately, he stayed in the doorway after putting the plate down on the table, looking from Kelly to me with a sympathetic expression.

"You both looked so serious when I came in," he said gently. "It's far too pretty a day for worries or conspiracy theories, don't you think?"

I stiffened. *Conspiracy theories?* Had he listened to our conversation?

Kelly waved him away. "We're fine, Dad," she said firmly, but with a smile. "We were just gossiping about the pageant. Teenage girls are allowed to gossip."

Kyle just smiled. "So you keep telling me." He turned and left the room. I listened to make sure his footsteps went all the way down the hall; they did.

As soon as Kyle left, Kelly's face turned thoughtful again. She picked up a brownie and toyed with it, breaking off a tiny piece and chewing it with a frown. "Nancy?" she said after a few seconds. "Can I tell you something?"

I looked up, surprised, and nodded. "Of course you can," I said encouragingly. "Anything. You know you can trust me."

Kelly sighed and continued picking at the brownie, focusing on it rather than me. "Remember what I told you about Portia back at the high school?"

I nodded. "Sure. What about it?"

"Everything I told you is true. She was a difficult Miss Pretty Face, and I didn't like her attitude, even back in the first rehearsals. But there's more." She glanced up at me hesitantly.

"What is it?" I asked. I knew Portia could be unpleasant—but what had she done to Kelly?

"Before Fallon dropped out," she went on, "the day before, we had a totally normal rehearsal. Fallon was in good spirits, really excited to win. Cupcake kept praising her and giving her little winks and stuff."

I nodded. "Okay."

"Afterward, I was a little late leaving, because I lost an earring and I went looking for it," Kelly continued. "I finally found it, but it took me at least twenty minutes to find it. When I got to the parking lot, I expected everybody to be gone.

But instead, over by the bleachers, I saw Portia and Fallon." She paused, meeting my eye. "I thought they barely knew each other. Had just met at the rehearsals, like all of us. But they were having what looked like a huge argument."

I leaned in. "An argument?" Kelly nodded. "What were they saying?"

"I couldn't hear." Kelly shrugged. "I mean, bits and pieces. I heard Fallon say, 'You couldn't.' And several times, I heard Portia say, 'Next year'—like that was a big deal. Portia had a folder with her, and she kept showing Fallon whatever was inside. Fallon looked *really* upset."

My mouth had dropped open. *Next year.* Like, *you can compete next year.* And the folder. What had it contained? Doctor's bills? Photographs?

Portia!

"The next day," Kelly went on, "Fallon dropped out. Just like that. And suddenly, Portia becomes the front-runner. And she went on to win." Kelly shook her head. "I don't know what their conversation was about. And I don't have proof it's related to Fallon leaving the competition. But ever since then, I *really* haven't trusted Portia." She paused, then bit into her brownie. "Maybe that's not fair of me. But it's true."

I grabbed a brownie and shoved it into my

mouth. I couldn't believe this. All this time I'd been working so hard to exonerate Portia, taking her abuse, and it seemed like . . .

"Can I ask you one more thing?" I asked, swallowing my brownie with a sip of soda. Kelly's earlier words were echoing in my mind. *Fallon had a plan, that she'd come out on top.* I had an awful feeling I had found the link between Fallon's blackmailing and Portia's dethroning.

"Sure," Kelly agreed.

"Does Fallon also know Candy Hokanson, your family friend? The owner of Fleur?"

Kelly frowned now, looking confused. "That's her aunt," she replied. "I mean, on her father's side, so she's not *my* aunt. But, Nancy . . ." She looked me in the eye, clearly upset now. "Why do you care about that? Why are you asking so many questions?"

I sighed. "Kelly," I said, realizing that once I made a move on my theories, my cover was about to be well and truly blown, "there's something I have to confess to you."

ALL'S FAIR IN LOVE AND PAGEANTS

"So this is a confrontation?" Ned asked me as we walked across the university campus together. Actually, we were following the same wooded path where I'd been so sure someone was following me the other night—a theory that was looking pretty unlikely now. We were on our way to meet Portia for dinner at the Seaver Hall cafeteria. Normally I would meet with her alone, but I was bringing Ned along this time because I was pretty sure she'd be unhappy with my news.

"More or less," I agreed with a sigh. "When I told Portia my suspicions about Fallon, she seemed upset. At the time, I thought it was just because she didn't think it was related to her dethroning. But now I realize the truth. Portia had some sort of angry confrontation with Fallon one night after rehearsal, and by the next morning, Fallon had dropped out of the competition? When she was the front-runner and had been gung-ho about pageants her whole life? Sounds shady to me."

Ned nodded. "So you think Portia blackmailed Fallon."

"To make her drop out of the competition," I added. "So that she could get the crown and the prizes, and Fallon could compete this year, when she'd still be eligible."

Ned shook his head in disbelief. "Wow."

I paused on the path. "Do you think I'm crazy?" I asked. "Do you know something about Portia that would prevent her from being a blackmailer? I almost wish you did. I would give anything to avoid this conversation."

Ned was still shaking his head. He gave me a comforting look. "No, don't be silly," he said. "This may not be pretty, but as usual, your hunch sounds right on. Portia does seem a little . . . aggressive. Willing to do anything to get what she wants. I just feel terrible for getting you involved in this case. All this time, you were working for a blackmailer." Ned frowned. "Wait, so who's responsible for setting up Portia? Or do you think she actually stole those dresses?"

I shook my head. "No, that's the crazy thing. Portia *didn't* steal those dresses. She was telling the truth about that; she just left out a very important part of her getting the crown in the first place. Fallon may be planning to win Miss Pretty Face this year, but I don't think that means she's forgiven and forgotten. I think she was furious about losing out *last* year and she wanted to see Portia get her due. So she went to her aunt— who just happens to be the owner of Fleur—"

"And she set Portia up," Ned finished. "Wow, Nance. These pageants are *crazy*, aren't they?"

I nodded. "To be honest with you, right now I can't wait to lose Miss Pretty Face and be done with the whole thing."

Ned sighed. We had reached Seaver Hall, and hungry students were flooding inside. The two of us, though, were hesitating. I wasn't looking forward to confronting Portia, and I don't think Ned was either.

"I guess we'd better go in," Ned said.

"I guess so." I gave Ned a hesitant look, and he took my hand in his and began walking to the entrance.

"I promise you, Nance," he said with a wry

smile, "the next client I throw your way won't be this crazy."

"What? WHAT?" Portia looked furiously from me to Ned and back, then stood up, shoving her chair back from the table. "WHAT did you just say?"

All around us, students turned from their chicken dinners to face the three of us. Portia glared down at the two of us, her mouth pulled into a taut line.

"I said," I replied quietly, shooting apologetic looks to our fellow diners, "that I know who blackmailed Fallon last year. I know it was you, Portia."

Portia shook her head, slowly settling back into her chair. "Not only is that preposterous, it has nothing to do with the case I hired you to solve."

"Portia, witnesses saw you fighting with Fallon in the parking lot that afternoon," I went on in a low voice. "They saw you showing her a folder, and her getting visibly upset while you kept saying 'next year.' Everyone knows that Fallon was the front-runner. And now *I* know that you blackmailed her to drop out of the competition or you'd expose the fact that she'd had a nose job." I paused. "You went on to win the competition. You thought it had worked out for you."

Portia was staring at me in disbelief. "Who saw me in the parking lot?"

I looked away. "That's not important. It all makes sense, Portia. You might as well just tell me you did it, because it relates to your getting set up."

Portia stared at me a long time, like she was trying hard to not believe me. Finally, though, she spoke. "All right. Maybe I did do it."

Out of the corner of my eye, I saw Ned shaking his head.

"I don't see why it matters," Portia went on. "Fallon and I have known each other forever. We weren't close friends, but we went to St. Claire's together—you know, the elementary school across town."

I nodded. St. Claire's was a small private school that went up to sixth grade. Most of its students joined the public school system in middle school, but the St. Claire's kids always seemed to have a special bond, since there were so few of them.

"Fallon was always so pretty, but she had this kind of funny, droopy nose. We used to make fun of it when we were little. Calling her Banana Nose and stuff."

I cringed. I got the feeling that by "we," Portia meant "I." Despite myself, I felt a little bad for Fallon.

"When she was gone for so long one February, I wondered what she could be doing. And then when she came back . . ." Portia looked down at her dinner, laughing. "I couldn't believe it! The surgeon she went to was great, and it was subtle. But are you kidding? Did she think I wouldn't notice her Banana Nose was gone? Please!"

"Did you confront her then?" I asked.

Portia shook her head. "Why bother? I just made note of it. And when I heard about the Miss Pretty Face pageant and all the prizes you could win, I signed up. I'd never been in a pageant before, but I wanted that scholarship. And I figured, hey, if Banana Nose could place in beauty contests even *before* she got it shaved off, I'd have a pretty good shot!" She chuckled to herself. "But when I signed up, Fallon was there. And she had the experience. And she did great in all of the rehearsals and competitions. *And* she had the new nose." Portia shook her head. "It made me crazy. As long as Banana Nose was in the competition, I didn't have a chance."

"So you blackmailed her," I supplied.

Portia glared at me. "Not right away," she said.

"I was reading some of the materials they gave us at home one night, and I noticed one of the conditions for competing: You *can't* have, or have ever had, plastic surgery. And I knew I had my shot."

Ned sighed. "You don't seem at all ashamed about this," he observed.

Portia stiffened. "Why should I be? *Fallon* broke the rules. I didn't set *her* up. She did it to herself. Actually, I cut her a break. I could have reported her to the pageant officials, but I didn't. I gave her the option of dropping out. I got the crown, she got to compete in this year's pageant—everybody wins!"

I laid down my fork. "I don't think Fallon sees it that way," I told Portia.

She looked at me curiously.

"Fallon's aunt is the owner of Fleur," I continued. "And Fallon told Kelly after she dropped out that she 'had a plan'—that she would still come out on top." I paused. "Are you following me? A girl who has a legitimate motive to hurt you, or at least to mar your reputation, is related to the woman who brought you down."

Portia's eyes widened. "*Fallon?*" she asked. "You think *Fallon* set me up to be dethroned?"

I glanced at Ned, not responding. I could see

Portia's face going through the information: confusion, then understanding, and then . . . *anger*.

"Oh my God," Portia breathed, shoving her dinner away. "Oh my God. That little rat. That little banana-nosed wannabe!"

"Portia," I cautioned, "you *did* . . ."

"Blackmail her, okay, all right, you said that already!" Portia grabbed her paper napkin off her tray and squeezed it in her fist. She looked from Ned to me, looking us both straight in the eye. Her expression was intense and, honestly, a little scary. "That doesn't change the fact that Fallon *took my crown*! I earned that crown fair and square, because Fallon did something against the rules! I was doing her a favor by not telling the officials! I *told* you that!"

I nodded. "I know that, Portia, but—"

"I might have to *leave school*!" Portia continued. "Or work, like, three jobs at a time! Not to mention the cash I lost, or the car, or the chance to be the face of Pretty Face Cosmetics! Do you have any idea what that position can lead to? Do you know how many starlets or models got their start as Miss Pretty Face?"

I started to shake my head. Just then, a familiar figure swooped in to clear Portia's untouched food. Robin Depken's concerned expression as she turned to Portia told me that she had over-heard the tail end of her rant.

"Listen to me," she said, looking Portia in the eye. "Whoever did that to you did you a favor. You don't want to work for those people. Trust me. I would never use their cosmetics on my face again."

Portia listened for a second, but then her face twisted into a sneer. "Spoken like a true has-been," she growled. "How would you know, Robin? You weren't good enough to get any-where near the crown."

Ned poked my arm and widened his eyes, no doubt thinking, as I was, that this was going to turn even nastier very soon. But Robin just stared at Portia, her concerned expression never chang-ing. "Whatever," she murmured, walking off with Portia's tray.

Portia turned back to me. Some of her anger seemed to have faded, and there were tears in her eyes. "I just can't believe what Fallon took from me," she said quietly. "What can I do to her? How can I—"

"If you're talking about revenge, I don't think it'll be necessary," I interrupted. "I have to tell the pageant officials everything I've learned. And once they learn that Fallon not only had plastic surgery but set you up to be dethroned, she's going to be in a ton of trouble."

Portia nodded, getting a gleam in her eyes. "And then they'll give me the crown back."

Ned looked alarmed. "Um," he spoke up. "They may not look kindly on you blackmailing a fellow contestant."

But Portia waved his concern away. "It's so *minor*, compared to what she did." She looked at both of us. "You guys don't see it because you're goody-goodies. You probably hear the word *blackmail* and break out in hives. But the pageant officials will see I just made an agreement with her. Besides, all's fair in love and pageants."

I looked at Ned and shook my head. "So I'm learning."

CONFRONTATIONS

The next day was the Miss Pretty Face pageant. But I no longer viewed it as anything to look forward to. For one, I was exhausted. After dinner, I'd made what was supposed to be a "quick" stop by Fleur to speak with Candy Hokanson. Luckily, she'd been there—and hesitantly, uncomfortably, and only after I'd laid out everything I already knew, she'd confirmed my suspicions about Fallon.

"Fallon is my niece," Candy had told me, staring at the floor. "She wanted that crown so badly. I tried to talk her out of it, but she insisted—she said Portia was a terrible person, and I'd be doing the pageant a favor."

I sighed. As relieved as I was to finally have

everything figured out, I was disappointed, too—in Portia, in Fallon, and in the adults who had gone against what they knew was right for silly, petty reasons. I couldn't help but wonder if all pageants were this scandal-ridden. I knew I'd never be competing in one again.

"Do you have to tell them?" Candy had asked me, looking at me with wide, childlike eyes. Oddly enough, she looked frightened. "Fallon is a good girl. If she says Portia had it coming, then she had it coming. Fallon's never lied to me."

I shook my head. "I have to tell them."

"But what good would it do?" Candy pressed. "You said Portia blackmailed Fallon. Both she and Fallon are at fault, and Portia can't get the crown back now." She looked me in the eye. "Just let it go," she coaxed. "Everyone will be better off."

I just looked at her, regretfully. "I can't."

"Why?"

"Because it's the truth."

Candy just pursed her lips and walked away. "We're closed," she'd told me bluntly, pointing me to the door.

This morning, Portia had agreed to meet me at nine thirty a.m. in front of the auditorium. Pageant contestants wouldn't arrive until ten, but that gave us plenty of time to explain the situation to the judges. As usual, Portia looked flawless: perfectly styled hair, perfectly applied makeup, and wearing glossy-magazine-style clothes.

"I can't wait to go in there," she greeted me as I climbed out of my SUV. "I've been waiting months for this: my big chance to show them I never stole anything."

Remembering what Kelly and Candy had told me, I couldn't help wondering what Portia *had* done. She hadn't stolen anything, but she *had* been rude (at least according to Kyle), irresponsible, and selfish during her reign, even though she'd won "fair and square," as she put it. It made me wonder: What do beauty contests measure, if people like Kelly are passed over so people like Portia can win?

Cupcake was already in the auditorium, supervising the stagehands as they arranged the platforms and lights. "Over to the left!" she was yelling as Portia and I entered at the rear. "Honestly, how many times do I have to tell you people? Don't apologize! Just *do it right*!" She turned, her jaw dropping as she saw Portia and I heading down the aisle toward her. "What the . . . ?"

"Cupcake, I have something to confess to you," I said quickly. "I am not just a hopelessly uncoordinated, style-deprived pageant contestant from River Heights." I paused. "Well, I guess I *am*—style-deprived and uncoordinated, I mean. But I'm also an amateur detective." I gestured to Portia. "And I've been competing in this pageant as part of my investigation for Portia."

Cupcake stared at Portia in awe. "Portia Leoni," she said in a low voice. "You have some nerve, walking in here, tainting the set of the pageant you made into a local joke!"

"Careful what you say to me, Cupcake," Portia replied with a cold smile. "You don't want to have to spend all day apologizing."

Cupcake gasped. "Well, I never!"

"Listen," I said, trying to prevent this from becoming a scene. "I have some information that the pageant officials need to hear. Can you arrange a meeting?"

Cupcake frowned, looking from me to Portia—probably her two least favorite people associated with the Miss Pretty Face pageant. She looked like she didn't want to believe us—but she did. "All right," she said finally. "I'll collect the pageant officials. You wait here."

Cupcake walked up onto the stage and into the backstage area, pausing to glare back at us every few seconds.

"Wow," Portia said with a chuckle, once Cupcake was out of hearing range. "She *really* hates me."

"Well, you brought scandal to what I think is the most important event in her life," I replied.

Portia just shook her head. "She doesn't seem to like you much either."

"I thought I'd been impressing her lately." I sighed. "But by showing up with you? I think I just lost my shot at Miss Congeniality."

A few minutes later Portia and I sat in a room with Cupcake, Kyle McMahon, and a few other local bigwigs from Pretty Face Cosmetics I hadn't met before: an older man named Henry Schafer, who introduced himself as a regional sales manager, and a middle-aged woman named Lucille Gomez, who was the company's PR representative.

All of these people eyed Portia and me suspiciously. I was beginning to sense that it wasn't just Cupcake who didn't like me.

"I do wish, Nancy," Kyle began, "that if you'd had information about Portia's shoplifting charge, you would have told us earlier. We don't appreciate being ambushed on the day of our next pageant."

"I'm not trying to ambush you," I replied honestly. "The truth is, the information I have about Portia's dethroning relates to this year's competition."

"And why is that?" Lucille asked skeptically.

"Because it involves one of this year's competitors," I replied.

I told them what I'd learned about Fallon Gregory and how that had led me to investigate her leaving the competition.

"And you *admit* that you blackmailed Fallon last year?" Cupcake demanded of Portia, her nose wrinkled in distaste.

Portia nodded. "As I've explained to Nancy," she replied, "I don't see it as a problem. I could have turned her in and then she would have been out of the competition for life. Wasn't it nicer of me to let her compete this year?"

Kyle shook his head and sighed. "I can't believe this," he murmured. "Fallon is my niece, and she didn't breathe a word of this to anyone."

Portia nodded. "She didn't realize that plastic surgery wasn't allowed," she went on confidently. "She had kept the nose job super-secret, so only her parents knew. When I told her the situation, she actually seemed grateful. You know, that I would warn her, and not turn her in to you officials." She paused, her brows furrowing. "But then with Nancy's help, I found out the truth! *Fallon* was the one who broke the rules, but she wanted revenge on me!"

Henry Schafer pursed his lips in disgust, as though he found Portia's outburst to be in poor taste. "What are you saying?"

"I'm saying that Fallon Gregory set Portia up to be dethroned," I cut in smoothly, wanting to keep Portia as quiet as I could. I laid it all out for them: Candy's strange behavior when I'd visited Fleur; the salesgirl's news that the store had been in danger of closing; Fallon's comment to Kelly that she would "come out on top"; and, finally, Candy's confession. "Fallon wanted revenge on Portia. They've known each other since they were little, and have never gotten along. Of course Fallon resented her old rival blackmailing her out of the crown she thought she deserved."

The pageant officials looked dumbfounded. I could tell they'd all grown accustomed to thinking of Portia as a liar and a thief, and her admission that she'd blackmailed Fallon only added to that reputation. Still, what I was saying made sense. They glanced at each other uncomfortably, as though deciding what to do.

"Are the contestants here yet?" Lucille asked Cupcake.

Cupcake glanced at her watch. "Oh, heavens, yes," she replied, jumping up. "I should go and tend to them. Whatever happened last year"—she stopped to glare at Portia—"we still have a pageant to put on."

Kyle held up his hand. "Just a minute, Cupcake," he said with a sigh. When all eyes turned to him, he looked gravely at me and Portia. "I think you'd better tell Fallon to come in here. I'm going to place a call to Fleur."

Twenty minutes later, we were all assembled. A few yards away, the dressing area for the Miss Pretty Face contestants was buzzing with girls shimmying into their dresses and smearing on their Pretty Face makeup. But in the small empty classroom we occupied, you could hear a pin drop. Fallon had finally stopped gasping and whining about why she was called in, and now sat quietly between Kyle and her aunt Candy, who had just arrived. Candy looked upset. The two hadn't exchanged a word except for "hello."

Finally Kyle broke the silence by clearing his throat. "Nancy," he said, "would you like to tell everyone here what you've told us?"

I took a deep breath as all eyes turned to me. "I believe Portia was set up to be dethroned as Miss Pretty Face," I said simply. "And I believe Fallon Gregory was behind it."

Fallon's face went chalk white as her mouth dropped open in alarm "*What?* Are you—are you crazy?!"

But Kyle hushed her. "Wait for Nancy to finish, please."

I laid it all out for the second time. The plastic surgery; Portia blackmailing Fallon; the shoplifting scam and Fallon's connections to Fleur. As I spoke, Fallon's face remained frozen in shock. Her beautiful features turned ugly with shock and rage. She looked furiously from me, to Portia—and then, finally, to Candy.

"It's not true," she insisted. "I would never. It's not true, tell them, Auntie Candy."

But Candy only looked miserably at her lap. She was silent. Portia shot me a triumphant expression, unable to hide her grin.

"*Auntie!*" Fallon cried, sounding angry now. "Tell them! Tell them I didn't do it!"

Candy stayed still for a few seconds, then sighed and closed her eyes. "I can't, Fallon," she said quietly. "Because it *is* true."

"Ha!" Portia cried, unable to contain herself

any longer. "It's *true*, Fallon, you know it is! You couldn't stand that I'd won the crown you'd lost with your stupid nose job—so you *took* it from me! You have some nerve! I hope you're banned from beauty pageants for the rest of your life! I hope your *nose job* reverses and you get your awful Banana Nose back! You deserve it!"

I reached over and grabbed Portia's arm. "Cool it," I whispered.

But Fallon didn't even seem to hear Portia's rant. She was already crying. Dark Pretty Face mascara streamed down her face with her tears as she looked from me to Candy. "I can't believe this," she said quietly. "I can't believe it. I can't . . ."

"Fallon," said Kyle. "I'm afraid . . ."

"*No!*" Fallon sobbed.

"You've broken several of the conditions for competing in Miss Pretty Face, and I'm afraid that you're disqualified from the current and all future competitions."

Fallon shook her head, sobbing. "No! No! I was supposed to *win* this year!"

Candy was still staring down at her lap. She sat tensely, like she would give anything to get out of this room.

"As for you." Kyle turned to Portia, who grinned eagerly. "On behalf of Miss Pretty

Face, I apologize for the treatment you received during and after the shoplifting scandal. I see now that you were innocent. And I'm sorry for any . . . embarrassment we caused you."

Portia just kept grinning. "Oh, it's all right, you didn't know," she said, pausing, obviously waiting for him to continue. But Kyle turned away and rubbed his eyes tiredly. All attention seemed to turn back to the sobbing Fallon.

Portia glanced at me, a confused look on her face.

"Um, excuse me," she said, an edge creeping into her voice. "But I was a lot more than *embarrassed* by those accusations. I lost my scholarship, my car, my livelihood. You're going to reinstate me, aren't you?"

Kyle turned around, and Lucille and Henry exchanged concerned glances. Kyle looked at Portia and frowned.

"*Reinstate* you?" he asked. "Reinstate you? No, I'm afraid I can't do that, Portia. You may not have shoplifted, but we've now learned that you blackmailed a fellow contestant into dropping out of the competition." He glanced at Fallon, who was wiping her eyes with Henry's handkerchief. "Isn't that right, Fallon?"

Fallon nodded slowly. "Yes." She glared at Portia. "She said if I didn't drop out, she'd get me *kicked* out."

Portia's eyes narrowed. "And to you, that was a good enough reason to send me to jail," she replied.

"You didn't go to jail," I pointed out.

Portia glanced at me in surprise, like she'd forgotten I was there. "Only because Candy felt guilty and dropped the charges," she hissed, drawing closer to me. "So, just to recap: I lost my crown, my scholarship, my car, *everything,* and then I hired you to fix it, and instead you got me thrown out on some other charge."

"You—" I started to defend myself, but stopped. The case was over. What was the point?

Portia glared at me one last time, then turned on her heel and walked out. "Thanks for nothing, Nancy Drew."

The door slammed behind her.

For a few seconds there was silence, except for Fallon's sobbing.

"Nancy," Kyle said finally, gently. "I appreciate your bringing this to my attention. But perhaps you should go get ready."

My head snapped up. "Ready?" I asked.

"For the *pageant*," Lucille added.

I turned to Kyle. "But I—I mean, I thought it was clear—"

"I know you were competing for your investigation," Kyle explained with a warm smile, "but I think you learned more than just scandal. When I saw your rehearsal yesterday, I was struck by your poise and talent. I think you should compete in the pageant, Nancy. I think you have a shot at the crown."

Fallon sobbed harder. Candy glanced up at me, looking uncomfortable. Henry and Lucille stared at me curiously. Suddenly, I think I would have done anything to get out of that room.

"Okay," I said quickly. "I'll go put on my dress!"

MISS PRETTY FACE

There I was, decked out in a sequined flamingo dress, with my hair teased and twisted into a complicated updo that Bess called "the Parisian rose." It was fifteen minutes till curtain. Bess flittered around me, adjusting my dress, clipping on earrings, mixing lipstick shades on her hand to find "the ultimate rosy-pink," as she put it. George was leaning against my dressing table, watching the proceedings with an amused smirk. "I cannot *believe* I left my digital camcorder at home," she said with a sigh.

"George?" I replied as Bess applied yet another coat of hair spray. "If I see this pageant on YouTube, I will spill a whole can of soda on your laptop."

George ignored me, shifting to get a better look. "Is that a *flamingo*?"

"Special delivery for Nancy Drew!" Cupcake chirped, sweeping into my area with a huge bouquet of pink roses. She glanced at me approvingly and gave me a warm smile. It seemed like she'd gotten past her anger at my disrupting the pageant once she realized that my charges against Fallon were true.

"Ohhh, how beautiful," Bess cooed.

I reached into the middle and pulled out the card that came with the flowers, reading it aloud: "'Best of luck to our favorite pretty face. Love, Dad and Ned.'" I smiled. Dad and Ned were sitting together in the audience.

"That's sweet," George admitted.

"Very!" squealed Bess. "Oh, Nance, you look so gorgeous. I just know you're going to win this thing."

I laughed. "That's because you haven't seen the other contestants."

Cupcake, who was lingering by my dressing area, checked her watch. "Oh my, look at the time. Nancy, I'm afraid your friends will have to leave. All non-contestants must take their seats in the audience."

I turned to my two best friends. "You heard her."

George and Bess looked me over, both smiling encouragingly.

"You know," said George, "I still think pageants are a humiliating way to exploit women, but you do look amazing, Nancy."

"Do you ever!" Bess added with a grin.

"Thanks, guys." I smiled. "I couldn't have done it without you. And I'll see you after the pageant, just as soon as I lose and scrape all this makeup off my face."

Bess laughed. "Don't say that too loud, Nancy," she said, picking up her purse and heading to the exit with George. "This is sponsored by a *cosmetics* company!"

I waved them off, pausing to look at myself in the mirror. I had to admit they were right: With Bess's hair and makeup job and all the sequins, I looked completely different. Glowy. Confident. I smiled at my reflection, and had to admit I looked pretty great. Not that I would *ever* wear this dress or hairdo again—but it was nice to know I had a sparkly side.

"Hey!" I called, spotting a familiar face going by in the mirror. "Piper!"

Piper turned and glanced at me. She looked stunning: Her dark golden hair was styled in loose, dangling curls, and a sparking violet gown set off her tanned skin and dark eyes. Rhinestone chandelier earrings dazzled her earlobes, drawing attention to her perfectly drawn pink lips.

She sighed. "*What?*"

Hmmm. It seemed like Piper had taken the disqualification of her best friend kind of badly.

"Look, I just wanted to say I'm sorry." I moved closer, smiling apologetically. "I took Portia's case because I didn't think she should be dethroned unfairly. I had no idea the trail would lead to Fallon, or that it would end with her being disqualified."

Piper looked at me in confusion. "What?" she snapped. "Oh, right, the investigation thing. Fallon said something about that. What are you, some kind of detective?"

I shrugged, surprised by the edge in her voice. "Some kind," I agreed.

Piper sighed and tossed her hair over her shoulders. "Look, if you think you broke my heart by getting Fallon kicked out, you're wrong. That's just one less girl standing in my way. Okay?"

I stepped back, stunned. Where was the sweet Piper who called me "girl" and brought me lemonade? "Okay."

Piper glanced at me out of the side of her eyes. "And good for you, for competing or whatever.

But let's get one thing straight. With Fallon out of the competition, that crown is mine. And we're not friends again until I'm wearing it. Got it?"

I nodded, too stunned to speak. "Got it," I whispered finally.

"Good." Piper turned on her heel and sashayed toward the stage, where the contestants were starting to line up.

Deirdre stepped away from her dressing area, adjusting her strap nervously. She, too, looked amazing in her beaded pink sheath, with her hair swept up in curls and a pink rose tucked into the middle.

"Hey, Deirdre," I called.

She glanced over, looking me up and down. "Hey, Nancy," she replied, a reluctant smile forming on her lips.

"You look beautiful," I said honestly.

Deirdre nodded slowly. "You too," she said quickly. Then she shuffled off toward the stage.

I sighed, taking one last look at myself in the mirror. This is it. In a way I couldn't wait to get out on stage and lose this thing so I'd never have to think about pageants again. All of the backstabbing and the lies were making me dizzy. Portia and Fallon had both gone crazy for the crown—and now Piper? Who next? Was anybody who competed in pageants sane?

I headed over to the backstage waiting area and smiled as I spotted the one sane person here: Kelly. Kelly was wearing her beautiful peacock dress with her hair up in a French twist and her sparkling tiara on her head. Ever since I'd told Kelly that I was investigating the pageant, she'd been a little distant with me: not mean, but she didn't seem quite sure whether she could trust me or not. "I know you're a good person, Nancy," she'd told me as we'd said our good-byes at lunch the day before. "I just . . . need some time to process this. That's all."

Now I caught her eye and smiled, giving her a little tentative wave. To my great relief, a huge smile took over her face and she laughed, opening her arms wide in surprise. "Look at you! My gosh, Nancy, you look like a bona fide pageant girl."

The contestants were already lining up, and Cupcake was going down the line, checking to make sure that everyone was "pageant-ready." "Piper, you look lovely. Deirdre, very nice. Nancy . . ." She paused and looked at me. First, she looked impressed, but then concern blossomed in her eyes. "Nancy," she said with alarm, making me wonder if a third eye had somehow erupted out of my forehead. "Your skin is bland. You don't look shimmery and revitalized!"

It hit me. "Shoot!"

"You forgot your Perfect Face!" Cupcake cried.

I scrambled, trying to figure out the fastest way to get it on. My dressing area was the farthest from the stage, and we only had one minute to curtain. "I'll-I'll—"

A hand reached out and firmly grabbed my arm. "Nancy, use mine." It was Kelly. "My dressing station's right over there. It's in the box on the table. Hurry!"

"Thanks!" I squeezed Kelly's arm and then ran over to her dressing station. Behind me, the River Heights High School Orchestra was already playing the first chords of our entrance song. I grabbed the plain cardboard box that all of our Pretty Face cosmetics had come in, and dug through the lipsticks and pans of eyeshadow. At the bottom, I felt a small square box that had to be it. I pulled it out, tore open the box, and pulled out . . .

A white bottle?

I stared down at it, surprised.

PERFECT FACE, said the handwritten label. Where was the pretty pink tube, printed with an

English garden scene, that all the rest of the contestants had received? I scrambled to twist off the cap, and took a whiff.

VANILLA.

This was the test version.

Granted, Kelly got samples of early products from her dad all the time. And I'd seen this very version of Perfect Face in her room just days before. But we were all given boxes of new Pretty Face products, mailed straight from the factory, to use at the pageant. Why would Kelly replace her "real" Perfect Face with this early test version?

"*Nancy!*" shrieked Cupcake from the entrance to the stage. "Get your Perfect Face on and get out here, *now!* We've got twenty seconds till we start the procession!"

Shaking with nerves, I turned the bottle over and shook a dollop into my hand, then used my fingers to spread it on my face. The lotion was cool and refreshing, but there was something missing. *The tingle.* The strange sensation that I'd gotten every time I'd used my Perfect Face before was gone.

Suddenly Robin Depken's words came back to me. *I would never use their products on my face again.* A chill ran down my spine. *That pageant is the biggest joke in a town full of them. The real competition has nothing to do with you.*

What were Kelly and Kyle hiding?

"NANCY!" Cupcake screeched. "We're entering! *Now!*"

I dumped the bottle back on the table and ran, as best I could in my heels, over to the stage. Just as Deirdre, who was right in front of me in line, took to the stage, I slid in behind her. Passing my hand over my head to smooth back any stray hairs, I pasted on my best Vaseline smile and stepped into the lights.

I had a pageant to lose.

"And the winner," Kyle McMahon read off his card, "of this year's Miss Congeniality title, is . . ."

I braced myself. Since there was no way on earth I was winning this pageant—I'd been so distracted throughout the competition that I'd tripped during our entrance and forgotten key words to "On My Own"—I figured my only chance of being called out was for these lesser titles. I really didn't want to win anything, though. I wanted to get off this stage and do some real thinking about Perfect Face.

". . . Deirdre Shannon!"

"Oh my gosh!" Deirdre, still standing next

to me, squeezed my arm and shrieked. "Don't worry, Nancy," she whispered to me before she left, her usual haughty expression returning. "I'm sure you'll win *something*."

I just smiled. I watched as Kyle awarded Deirdre with a MISS CONGENIALITY sash. Miss Congeniality worked out pretty well for Kelly, I figured. Maybe Deirdre can take the crown after some big scandal hits.

"And now the runners-up!" Kyle paused and gave us all a meaningful look, letting us know that we were getting to the end. "The second runner-up is . . ."

I stifled a yawn.

"Julia Felice!"

Julia, a pretty brunette with short hair, stepped forward to accept her sash. Kyle then turned back to the audience. "The next name I call, the runner-up, is an important position, and will take over as Miss Pretty Face if the winner is unable to fulfill her duties."

A muffled titter went through the crowd—no doubt everyone was thinking back to the embarrassing Portia Leoni scandal, when the winner was unable to fulfill her duties.

"Our runner-up this year is . . . Piper Depken!"

My mouth dropped open. *Piper?* But that

meant . . . she hadn't won. And how was that possible? All of Cupcake's favorite girls—Deirdre, Julia, Piper, and Fallon—had all either placed already or had been disqualified. This was going to be a huge upset. Who, of the girls left, could reasonably win?

Piper was unable to hide her disappointment and anger as she walked up to Kyle at the front of the stage. When he fumbled with the sash, she grabbed it out of his hands and angrily threw it over her head.

"Congratulations," I heard him tell her.

But she just sneered and rolled her eyes.

Kyle ignored her, grinning hugely as he took the microphone again. "And that brings us up to the main event—this year's new Miss Pretty Face! My daughter, Kelly, has done an excellent job as Miss Pretty Face for the remainder of last year's term. As you may know, she's worked with terminally ill children and been a wonderful representative for her generation and for Pretty Face Cosmetics."

Kelly stepped forward at the mention of her name, walking a slow loop around the front of the stage as photos from her reign were projected behind her and the audience cheered. When she finished her loop, she stood quietly next to her father.

"As you know," Kyle said, as the lights dimmed and the drummer started drumming, "the Miss Pretty Face title doesn't just come with a crown. The winner will also receive a four-year scholarship to the institution of her choice; a new car, hers to keep even after her reign ends; a contract to be a spokesmodel for Pretty Face Cosmetics; and free Pretty Face Cosmetics for life!" Kyle paused, and the audience cheered again. "In addition, the winner will travel with me, Kelly, and Piper to compete in the national Miss Pretty Face pageant in New York City! We'll depart next week!"

The applause grew even louder. I squinted, trying to see Bess, George, Ned, and Dad in the audience. There they were: fourth row. Ned winked at me, and I winked back. *Don't go anywhere,* I wanted to say. *I'll be out of this makeup and out there soon.* I was anxious to talk to Ned about Kelly's suspect tube of Perfect Face. Something about it unnerved me, in the same way I had been unnerved in the parking lot when I thought someone had been following me. Could I have been right about that after all—had someone followed me? I was starting to feel like there was a bigger mystery behind this whole competition than Portia Leoni and her dethroning.

"This year's new Miss Pretty Face . . . is . . ." Kyle caught my eye. Why was he looking at me like that?

And then, in the instant before he said the name, I knew. My knees went weak. I felt like I might throw up.

"*Nancy Drew!*" The audience erupted into applause.

So many things happened at once. The music changed, and got louder. All of my fellow contestants ran over to hug me. Flashbulbs went off. Kelly broke out into a huge grin and started clapping.

Somehow, I don't know how, I made my way to the front of the stage.

Me? I won? But *how*?

I was vaguely aware of Kyle placing the sash around me, and Kelly gently removing the crown from her head and firmly bobby-pinning it to place onto mine.

"I was horrible," I whispered to her. "How did I win? How did Piper lose?"

Kelly just shrugged and smiled at me. "Enjoy it, Nancy. You'll make a great beauty queen."

I looked from her, to Kyle, to the audience.

For so long, I'd so wanted this pageant to be over. But, now—well, now it looked like I was headed to New York City for the next round of competition. I decided maybe that wasn't such a bad thing. There was something else going on with this pageant that had my detective senses tingling. And I had a feeling the next competition was going to be even more scandalous than the first.

I glanced over at Kyle and Kelly, both of them beaming at me. I returned their smiles, thinking about the vanilla Perfect Face and my skin, which still didn't feel the slightest bit tingly. Did Kyle and Kelly know something that the rest of us didn't?

One thing was for sure: I'd done it again. I had another mystery to solve—and this time, the subject was Pretty Face Cosmetics.

TO BE CONTINUED . . .